THIS BOOK BELONGS TO

EVAN

SCOOBY-DOO!™
STORYTIME SCREAM

CONTENTS

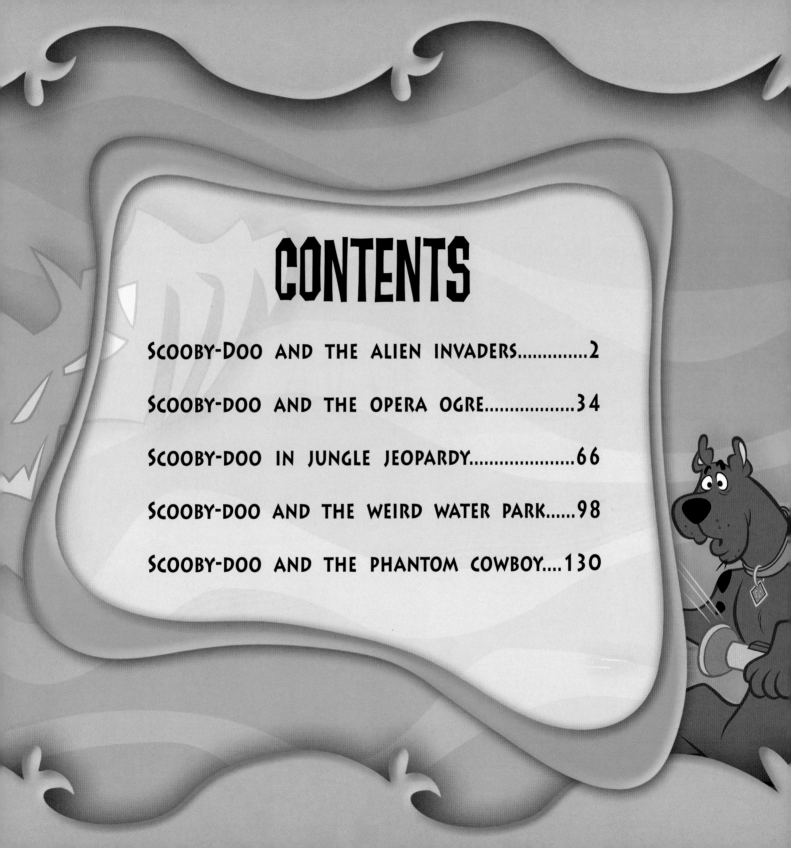

MEET THE GANG

WHETHER VAMPIRE STALKING, GHOST HUNTING OR DEMON BUSTING, THERE'S NO MYSTERY THAT THIS GROUP OF PALS CAN'T SOLVE!

SCOOBY

NAME: SCOOBERT (SCOOBY, SCOOB, SCOOBY-DOOBY-DOO)

ADDRESS: KENNEL BEHIND SHAGGY'S HOUSE

AGE: 7

HEIGHT: 12 PAWS

DRESS: TEAL COLLAR WITH DIAMOND SHAPED TAG

LIKES: SCOOBY SNACKS, PIZZA, ICE CREAMS

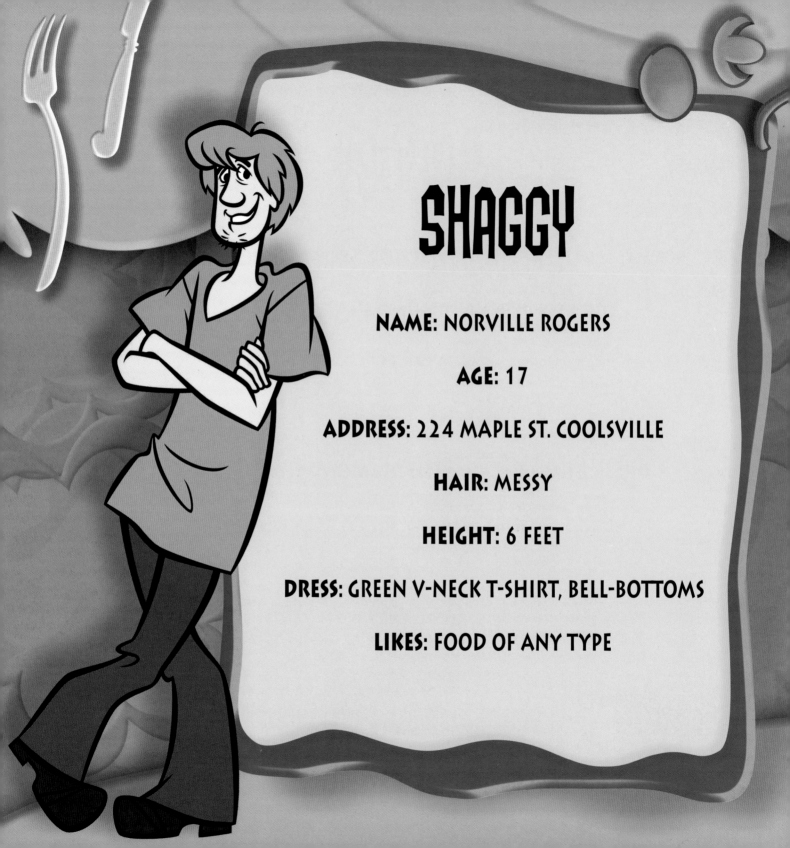

SHAGGY

NAME: NORVILLE ROGERS

AGE: 17

ADDRESS: 224 MAPLE ST. COOLSVILLE

HAIR: MESSY

HEIGHT: 6 FEET

DRESS: GREEN V-NECK T-SHIRT, BELL-BOTTOMS

LIKES: FOOD OF ANY TYPE

VELMA

NAME: VELMA DINKLEY

AGE: 15

ADDRESS: 316 CIRCLE DRIVE. COOLSVILLE

HAIR: BROWN

HEIGHT: 4'9"

DRESS: ORANGE SWEATER, PLEATED SKIRT, KNEE SOCKS, BLACK HORN-RIMMED GLASSES

LIKES: SCIENCE, DETECTIVE WORK

FRED

NAME: FRED JONES

AGE: 17

ADDRESS: 123 TUNA LANE. COOLSVILLE

HAIR: BLONDE

HEIGHT: 5'11"

DRESS: SWEATER, ASCOT TIE, SLACKS

LIKES: MONSTER BUSTING

DAPHNE

NAME: DAPHNE BLAKE

AGE: 16

ADDRESS: 9000 EASY ST. COOLSVILLE

HAIR: AUBURN

HEIGHT: 5'7"

DRESS: PURPLE MINI DRESS WITH MATCHING HAIRBAND, PINK STOCKINGS AND LIME GREEN SCARF

LIKES: FASHION, HAVING ADVENTURES

SCOOBY-DOO AND THE ALIEN INVADERS

Scooby and his pals from Mystery, Inc. were travelling through the desert in the Mystery Machine. But then a big sandstorm struck, and Shaggy had trouble driving.

"Like, I can't see a thing!" cried Shaggy as he accidentally turned down the wrong road.

The sandstorm was so thick, no one noticed a NO TRESPASSING sign they passed. Suddenly, the whole van was bathed in a bright light from above!

It looked like a giant spaceship! It whooshed by so fast, it spun the Mystery Machine around and around. Shaggy couldn't keep control, and the van ran into a cactus.

When Scooby and the gang climbed out, the ship was gone.

"What was that thing?" Velma asked.

"Was it some kind of jet?" wondered Daphne.

"Not like any jet I've ever seen," said Fred. "Did you see how fast it was?"

The van wouldn't start again. Fred suggested they walk to a nearby town for help.

"There's snakes and stuff out there in the desert!" Shaggy gulped.

"Reah! Rattlerakes. Ssssssss!" Scooby hissed. He and Shaggy decided to stay behind and guard the van. But as soon as the others were gone, they immediately started looking for Scooby Snacks. There was only one left!

They both grabbed for it, but it fell, bounced across the ground, and was picked up by a strange animal!

"Zoinks! A jackalope!" Shaggy exclaimed. "I thought those things were fake."

"Ree, roo!" Scooby agreed.

The jackalope hopped off with the Scooby Snack. Shaggy and Scooby ran after it.

"Hey, put that down!" Shaggy shouted.

They chased the jackalope to a nearby hill. It ran into a tunnel that glowed with an eerie golden light. As they peered in, Scooby and Shaggy got the strange feeling they were not alone. They turned around and got a big surprise!

"Raliens!"

Shaggy and Scooby raced away as fast as they could. Two scary-looking aliens followed right behind on their space cycles.

Shaggy and Scooby tried disguising themselves as a pair of cacti, but that didn't fool the aliens. The two friends ran up and down hills, but they couldn't lose the creepy space critters.

Finally, they knocked loose some big, flat stones and rode them like sleds down the hill. They slid all the way to the nearby town and left their pursuers far behind!

Shaggy and Scooby ran into the town diner. Fred, Daphne, and Velma were inside. Scooby and Shaggy told them all about their alien encounter.

Aliens? The rest of the gang didn't know what to think.

"They're real!" shouted a crazy-looking man named Lester. "Them aliens are here to take over the world!"

"Have you had some contact with aliens?" asked Velma.

"That's right," said Lester. "Took me aboard their ship, they did!"

Lester told them about his close encounter aboard the alien spaceship. Since the gang couldn't get the van to a mechanic until morning, he offered to let them spend the night at his place. Lester had all sorts of kooky alien stuff.

Daphne saw some satellite dishes through Lester's window. "What are those?" she asked.

"S.A.L.F. dishes," Lester explained. "The government put 'em up. S.A.L.F. means Search for Alien Life-forms. Ever since they built them dishes, aliens started showing up."

Lester didn't have a lot of room. Shaggy and Scooby had to sleep on his roof in a couple of lawn chairs, but they didn't mind.

"Hey! It's pretty groovy up here," Shaggy remarked.

"Ruh-huh!" Scooby agreed.

Soon they were fast asleep and snoring under a desert sky full of beautiful, twinkling stars.

But one of the lights twinkling overhead wasn't a star - it was a spaceship! It hovered over them, dropped claws down, and lifted them up inside!

Scooby and Shaggy didn't stir until they were strapped to the aliens' laboratory tables.

"Hey! Let us go!" Shaggy cried. "We taste terrible! Like, I'm all stringy."

Scooby was very scared, even though some of the experiments tickled.

"Do not fear us, earth creatures," said one of the aliens. "Cooperate and you will not be harmed."

But when the aliens weren't looking, Scooby used his tail to push a button that released him. He jumped up and ran away, pushing Shaggy's table as he went.

"Sorry, but our health plans don't cover exams!" Shaggy yelled as Scooby pulled him away.

The angry aliens chased them all over the spaceship. Shaggy and Scooby couldn't find a way out. Suddenly, a third alien appeared out of nowhere. They ran right into it!

This alien was much bigger than the other two. It pulled out an evil-looking device with all sorts of snapping blades and held it toward Scooby and Shaggy. They fainted dead away.

When they woke up, Shaggy and Scooby were back in the desert and the aliens were gone. They thought they were alone, but then they heard a voice.

"Hey, man, are you all right?"

The two friends couldn't believe their eyes. Standing in front of them was a pretty teenager named Crystal and her dog, Amber. They were the most beautiful girls Shaggy and Scooby had ever seen! Suddenly, the aliens didn't seem so important. In fact, Scooby and Shaggy thought the whole thing had been a nightmare.

"I'm a freelance photographer," Crystal explained. "I'm shooting some desert wildlife for a magazine."

Shaggy told Crystal about the jackalope and the aliens while Scooby showed off for Amber. Crystal asked Shaggy to show her where they'd seen the aliens and the jackalope.

As they walked toward Crystal's Jeep, Shaggy leaned over to Scooby. "Scoob, ol' buddy, I don't know about you," he whispered, "but I think I just found my dream girl."

"Ree, roo!" Scooby nodded.

After Fred took the Mystery Machine to a repair garage, he and the girls decided to check out the S.A.L.F. satellite dishes. They were given a tour by a big guy named Max and his coworkers, Laura and Steve.

"We're monitoring the cosmos twenty-four hours a day, seven days a week," Max explained.

Steve told them how boring the job was. They rarely heard or saw anything promising. But if there was even a tiny chance of making contact with aliens, it was worth it.

Meanwhile, Shaggy and Scooby showed Crystal and Amber the tunnel where they had followed the jackalope and had first seen the aliens. Suddenly, they were surprised by a gruff voice.

"What are you doing here?" Two military policemen appeared in front of them.

"Just taking some wildlife photos," Crystal told them.

"You aren't supposed to be here," said one of the policemen "This area is under government investigation."

The policemen checked Crystal's camera, then made them leave.

After they finished their tour of the satellite station, Fred, Daphne and Velma decided to check out a place called Scorpion Ridge. Max said the government had sent an investigation team there to look into reports about aliens.

They asked Lester to give them a ride to Scorpion Ridge. On the way there, Velma tried to figure things out. "Did you notice that Max, Laura, and Steve all had mud on their shoes?" she asked. "Where would there be mud around here?"

After the policemen had gone, Crystal wanted to go back to the strange tunnel. The boys didn't want to go, but when Crystal insisted, they reluctantly followed her and Amber inside.

It was really spooky inside the tunnel. Crystal guided the way with her flashlight as the tunnel led to a big cavern.

"I think I see something ahead," Crystal said.

"Like, the exit, I hope," gulped Shaggy as Scooby moaned in agreement.

Suddenly, they all stopped and gazed at the cavern walls in amazement.

Gold! The cavern walls were lined with gold!

"Scoob, ol' buddy, we've hit the jackpot!" Shaggy said excitedly. "We can buy our own food court!"

"Reah! Rooby Rhax, roo!" Scooby agreed, his eyes sparkling.

"Scooby Snacks?" Shaggy laughed. "With this much gold, we can buy a Scooby Snacks factory!"

"Reah! Reah!"

But their excitement didn't last long. Just then, two aliens jumped out at them. Once more, Shaggy and Scooby were running from the aliens - and this time Crystal and Amber were, too!

At the same time, Fred, Daphne, and Velma had made a discovery at Scorpion Ridge. They'd found the entrance to the gold mine, too - all sorts of mining equipment. In fact, they were surprised to see two military policemen operating the equipment.

Before they had much time to investigate, they were attacked by aliens. The aliens had lost Shaggy, Scooby, and their new friends, but now they had new victims!

The big alien chased Fred, Daphne, and Velma into a trap. Before they knew it, they were swept up into a net.

"You monsters!" cried Daphne.

"Silence, earthling!" said one of the smaller aliens. "You should not have interfered!"

Velma just smiled. "You can give up the hokey alien charade now . . . Steve."

The surprised alien slowly took off his mask. Sure enough, it was Steve from the satellite station. The alien next to him was Laura, and the big alien was Max.

Steve, Max, and Laura told them how they had discovered the gold mine and how they kept the locals away with the alien story. They built a phony spaceship out of a helicopter and hired a couple of friends to pretend to be military policemen.

"I knew it was all a fake!" said Fred.

"Well, it doesn't help you now," sneered Steve. He pulled a lever and the net swung over a deep, dark pit. Steve was going to drop them in!

The two policemen went in search of Shaggy, Scooby, Crystal, and Amber. Soon they found them and chased them to the edge of a cliff that dropped off into a dark abyss.

Shaggy and Scooby turned to face the big men. They started making karate movements to try and frighten the policemen. They were very pleased when the policemen suddenly looked scared, turned, and ran away.

They didn't realize that Crystal and Amber had transformed themselves. They were aliens!

Shaggy and Scooby chased the policemen all the way back to where the others were being held. Crystal and Amber had changed back to their human forms, so Shaggy and Scooby had no idea what had really scared the policemen.

"Like, stand aside, ladies," Shaggy said. "This is men's work."

"But, Shaggy . . ." Crystal started to warn him.

Before they knew what happened, Shaggy and Scooby were knocked to the ground by the big policemen. It wasn't a total loss - Fred, Daphne, and Velma used the diversion to escape!

Amber and Crystal were angry that their friends were being treated so roughly. So they transformed back into their alien forms. Fred, Daphne, and Velma couldn't believe their eyes.

"Jinkies!" exclaimed Velma.

Amber grabbed a steal girder and, using superhuman strength, twisted it around Max and the two big military policemen. They were trapped tight!

Shaggy and Scooby were just coming to when they glimpsed Amber and Crystal as aliens. They were so frightened they screamed.

Just as Velma was explaining who the aliens were, they heard a loud sound.

Suddenly, Steve appeared on a huge tractor. He was heading straight for Crystal and Amber! Crystal tripped and was about to be run over when Amber grabbed the tractor's shovel and bravely held back the machine.

But Amber wasn't strong enough to hold back the tractor for long. Everyone could tell that she was getting weaker and would soon lose her grip.

That's when Shaggy and Scooby-Doo saved the day! They drove in on another tractor, headed straight for Steve.

Scooby looked like he was a knight from the days of old, charging in with a lance to save his lady love. "Rooby-rooby-roo!" he roared.

Steve tried to back up his tractor and get away. But Shaggy sideswiped him and his tractor tumbled over!

"I don't believe it!" cried Steve, staring at Crystal and Amber.

"Come on, let's get out of here!" Laura yelled as she and Steve ran toward the mine's exit.

Fred jumped over to the control lever that held the net in the air. He flipped the switch and dropped it right on top of Steve and Laura. Now they were trapped, too.

"Yes!" cheered Fred.

Now that the mystery was solved and all the villains were captured, Amber and Crystal transformed back to their human forms.

"We were sent by our world to investigate signals from your planet," Crystal explained.

"Transmitted by the S.A.L.F. station," Amber added, and everyone gasped.

Shaggy looked at Amber. "You can talk?"

"Yes, quite well," Amber replied.

"Dig that, Scoob!" laughed Shaggy. "A talking dog!"

Suddenly there was a loud humming sound. A spaceship appeared above them, hovering over a hole in the cavern roof. It was the same ship the gang had seen during the sandstorm.

"Here's our ride," Amber said.

"We have to go," Crystal said as she hugged Shaggy good-bye. "I hope you can forgive us for deceiving you."

"Yeah, like, we understand," Shaggy replied.

"You are really a groovy guy, Shaggy." Crystal smiled and gave him a quick kiss.

Amber held Scooby's paws. "Good-bye, Scooby. I'll never forget you."

"Ree, roo, Ramber," Scooby said sadly.

The two aliens stepped into the light under the spaceship, waved one last good-bye, and were instantly gone.

Soon the FBI and the police had arrived to take the villains into custody. Max was trying to get the authorities to listen to him about the real aliens.

"We saw them!" Max was yelling as he was taken away. "They were big and . . ."

"Give it a rest, already!" muttered Steve. "No one's going to believe us."

Lester was there, smiling. He believed them.

The Mystery Machine was repaired and the gang was ready to leave, except for Shaggy and Scooby.

"You guys okay?" Fred asked them.

"Like, we're just completely destroyed, is all," Shaggy said sadly.

"Reah, restroyed," Scooby added.

Velma thought she had just the thing to cheer them up. She held up a new box of Scooby Snacks. Scooby and Shaggy jumped into the Mystery Machine and started gobbling up the Snacks.

"Well, that didn't take long!" Velma said, smiling.

As the van drove away across the desert, Shaggy and Scooby could be heard from a distance.

"Like, hey! It's mine!"

"Ro, rine!"

SCOOBY-DOO AND THE OPERA OGRE

"Awr-rooooooo!" howled Scooby-Doo.

"And, like, la-la-la-la Figaro! Figaro! Figaro!" sang Shaggy.

"All right, you two," Daphne scolded them. "Just because we're going to the opera doesn't mean you have to sing!"

Sure enough, the Mystery Machine was pulling up to a fancy theatre. But it looked like the opera house was on fire!

35

"Gee, what's going on here?" Velma asked as the gang climbed out of the Mystery Machine.

"Oh, it's terrible!" cried Mr. Samuels, the owner of the opera house. "Our entire production is ruined!"

All around Mr. Samuels, people were running out of the smoking opera house. There were audience members in fancy clothes, musicians in tuxedos, stage technicians all dressed in black, and performers in Viking costumes.

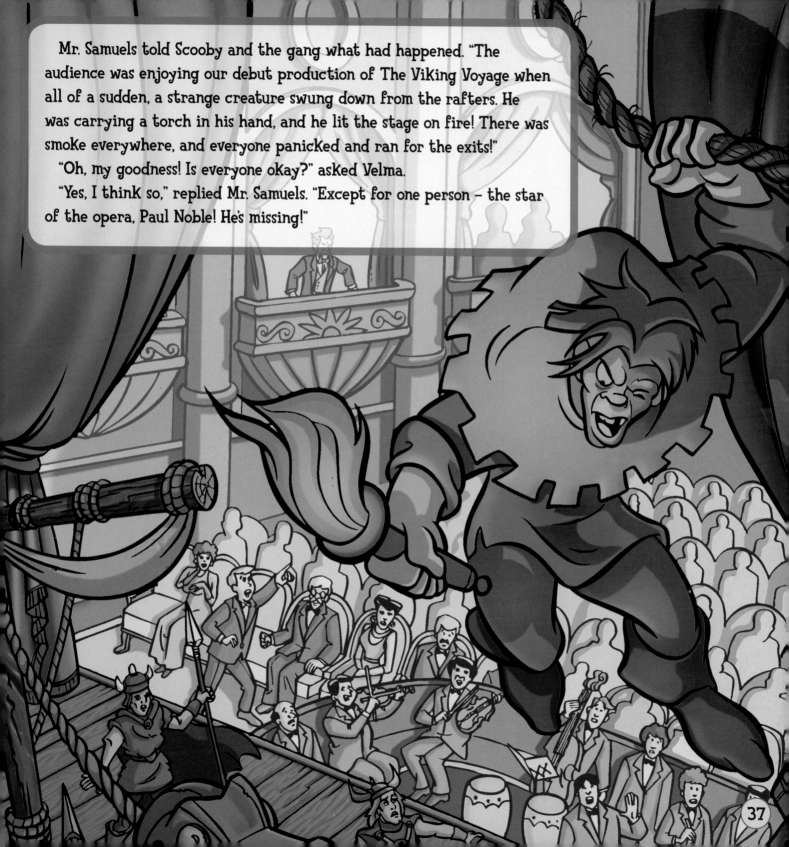

Mr. Samuels told Scooby and the gang what had happened. "The audience was enjoying our debut production of The Viking Voyage when all of a sudden, a strange creature swung down from the rafters. He was carrying a torch in his hand, and he lit the stage on fire! There was smoke everywhere, and everyone panicked and ran for the exits!"

"Oh, my goodness! Is everyone okay?" asked Velma.

"Yes, I think so," replied Mr. Samuels. "Except for one person – the star of the opera, Paul Noble! He's missing!"

One of the singers, a man named William Bluster, approached Mr. Samuels. "Don't worry, Samuels," Bluster said. "I can play the lead part. I am an expert in all things theatrical!" With a sniff he added, "Paul Noble probably went home. He's such a coward."

Mr. Samuels didn't know what to do. It was all so confusing. Then the firemen came out of the opera house looking puzzled.

There was no fire inside! Just a lot of smoke.

"Mr. Samuels, do you mind if we take a look inside?" Fred asked. "We're pretty good at solving mysteries like this."

Mr. Samuels was glad for the help. So the gang went inside, eager to find the cause of all the trouble. (Actually, Scooby and Shaggy were hoping to find a snack bar.)

No sooner had they entered the grand theatre than a creepy shadow appeared onstage.

"Stay away! Beware!" the shadow screamed. "Beware the wrath of the opera ogre!"

"Zoinks!" Shaggy cried. He and Scooby were so scared, they jumped into the orchestra pit. Shaggy ended up leaping headfirst into a big tuba.

"Like, help! I'm blind!" Shaggy hollered.

"Stop fooling around, you two," Velma chided.

Then something strange happened. When Scooby looked up at the gang from the orchestra pit, he realized that he was going down – and so was the whole pit!

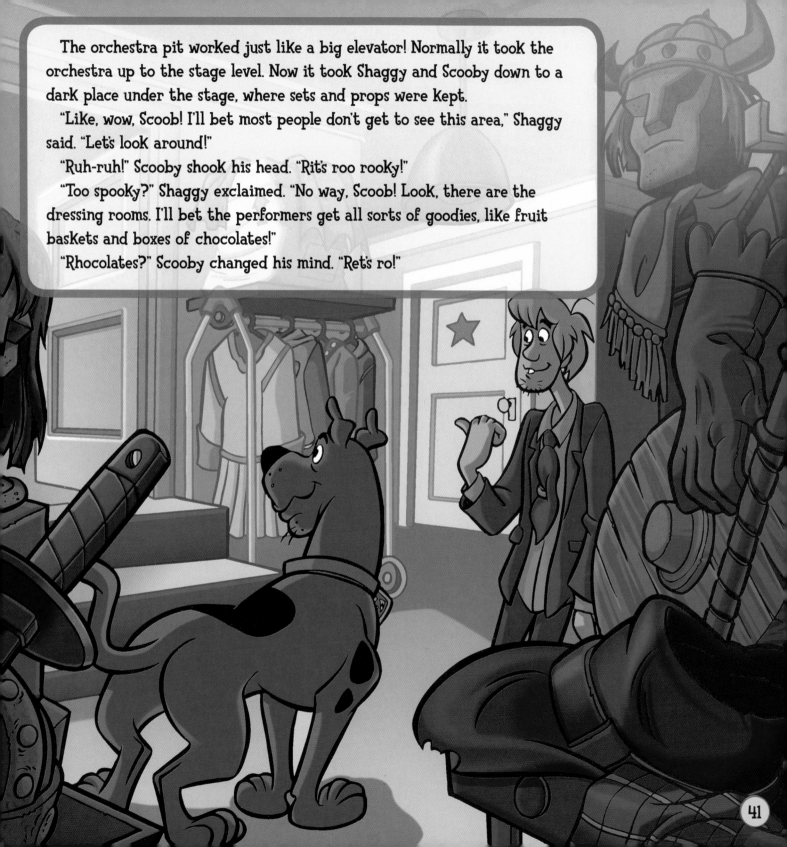

The orchestra pit worked just like a big elevator! Normally it took the orchestra up to the stage level. Now it took Shaggy and Scooby down to a dark place under the stage, where sets and props were kept.

"Like, wow, Scoob! I'll bet most people don't get to see this area," Shaggy said. "Let's look around!"

"Ruh-ruh!" Scooby shook his head. "Rit's roo rooky!"

"Too spooky?" Shaggy exclaimed. "No way, Scoob! Look, there are the dressing rooms. I'll bet the performers get all sorts of goodies, like fruit baskets and boxes of chocolates!"

"Rhocolates?" Scooby changed his mind. "Ret's ro!"

41

Scooby and Shaggy went into a dressing room with a gold star on the door. It belonged to the show's star, Paul Noble.

"Groovy, Scoob!" exclaimed Shaggy.

Scooby couldn't agree more. He sat at the makeup table and pretended he was a famous stage actor. He laughed at his reflection. "Ree-hee-hee!"

"Like, let's see what's in the closet," Shaggy said. Then he got a big scare!

"Rrrrrmmmm!" said the creature inside, reaching for Shaggy.

"Zoinks! It's a mummy!" Shaggy shouted.

Meanwhile, Fred, Daphne, and Velma were exploring the stage area. Off to the side of the main stage area was a place the audience couldn't see, called the "wings."

"This is where they keep the set pieces until they're ready to go onstage," Daphne explained. "And see those ropes? Those are used to raise and lower the scenery."

The kids were so busy looking at the scenery, they didn't see the creepy shadow of the opera ogre behind them on the floor – until it was too late!

43

Ka-boom! There was a fiery explosion, then out jumped the opera ogre!

"So! You have intruded on my domain, despite my warnings," the ogre said, his eyes glittering. "Now you must face my wrath!"

"Jinkies!" Velma exclaimed. "Let's get out of here! Exit stage left!"

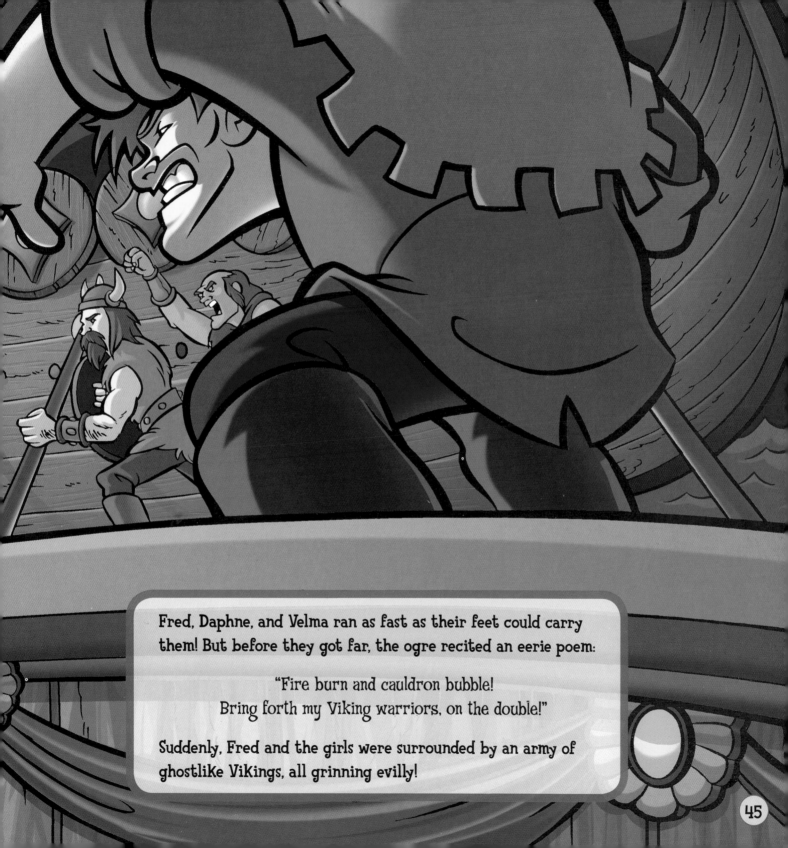

Fred, Daphne, and Velma ran as fast as their feet could carry them! But before they got far, the ogre recited an eerie poem:

"Fire burn and cauldron bubble!
Bring forth my Viking warriors, on the double!"

Suddenly, Fred and the girls were surrounded by an army of ghostlike Vikings, all grinning evilly!

The kids tried to get away, but they took a wrong turn.

"Jeepers!" Daphne shuddered. "This brings new meaning to the phrase 'stage fright'!"

"There's something strange about these Vikings," Velma remarked. "And we're going to get to the bottom of it."

Velma sounded brave, but it was hard not to shiver as the eerie Viking army crept closer!

In another part of the theatre, the mummy was chasing Shaggy and Scooby. The two friends ran through the theatre's green room with the mummy hot on their tail.

Every big theatre has a green room. It's the area where actors meet with audience members after a performance. Usually it's a very pleasant place to be. But right then, Scooby and Shaggy didn't find it pleasant at all! The mummy was gaining on them!

Luckily, Shaggy and Scooby were able to pull the old "one-two" on the mummy. The growling creature soon found itself sliding down a laundry chute.

"Like, make sure you use plenty of starch!" Shaggy called down the chute after the mummy.

Scooby got a big laugh out of that. Then he caught a glimpse of something exciting out of the corner of his eye!

"Rook, Raggy!" Scooby pointed.

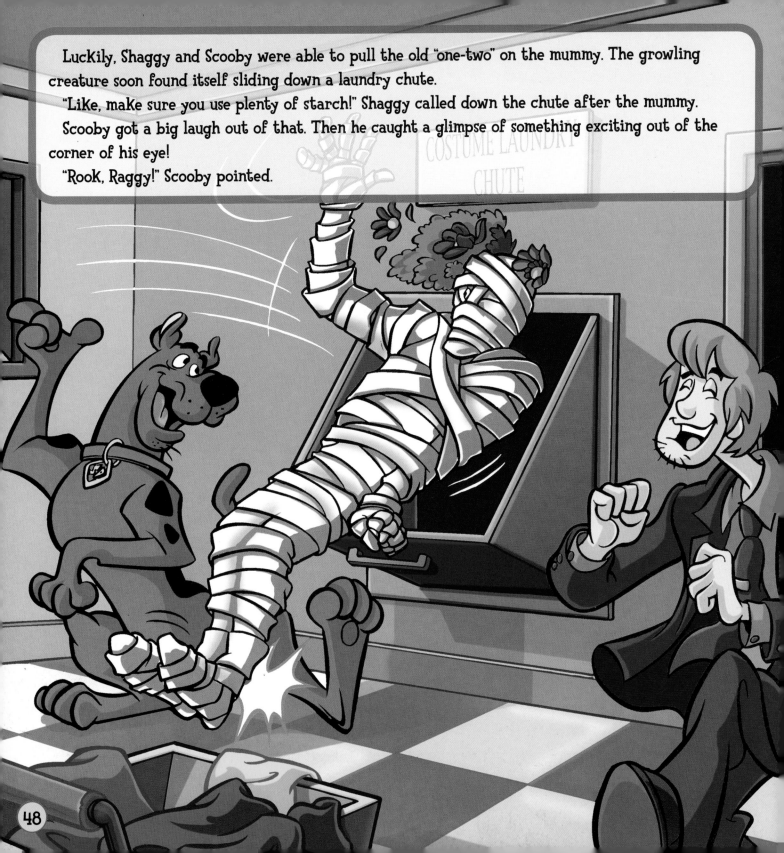

It was the costume room!

Shaggy and Scooby couldn't resist. They had to try on some costumes.

There were costumes of Kings, soldiers, cowboys, princesses, witches, and vampires!

"Like, we sure could have used disguises like these on some of our adventures!" Shaggy said as he dressed up as a fairy-tale princess. "Right, Scoob?"

"Ruh-huh!" Scooby agreed wholeheartedly, prancing around like a Roman general in battle.

Meanwhile, Fred, Daphne, and Velma were realizing something.

"Those Vikings haven't moved any closer," said Velma.

"And the opera ogre has disappeared!" Daphne added.

"Look!" exclaimed Fred. "These Vikings aren't ghosts after all. They're just big puppets."

The opera ogre had fooled the kids into thinking they were surrounded! Now he was off to cause mischief elsewhere in the theatre.

"C'mon, guys." Fred was heading offstage. "Let's see if we can't catch up with that tricky fellow!"

The kids soon found themselves in one of the dressing rooms. It was a big, long room where the chorus actors got ready before the show.

Daphne found a picture of the star, Paul Noble. Someone had drawn a funny face on it. "Boy, someone sure can't stand Paul Noble," she commented.

"Look at this. It could be a clue!" Velma exclaimed. She pointed at a container filled with smoke-making fluid used for special effects.

"And I found these long strips of canvas." Fred frowned. "What are these doing in the actors' dressing room?"

51

Upstairs, Shaggy and Scooby had run into a problem – an ogre of a problem!

Right in the middle of their play-acting, the opera ogre leaped into the costume room with a loud laugh.

"Flee now, or feel the wrath of the opera ogre!" he whispered menacingly.

"Zoinks! No need for wrath-ing, today, Mr. Creepy!" Shaggy cried as he and Scooby fled the room. "We're fleeing! We're fleeing!"

Scooby and Shaggy ran out to an area overlooking the stage. They came to a circular staircase used by the stage crew, and up they went. The opera ogre was close behind!

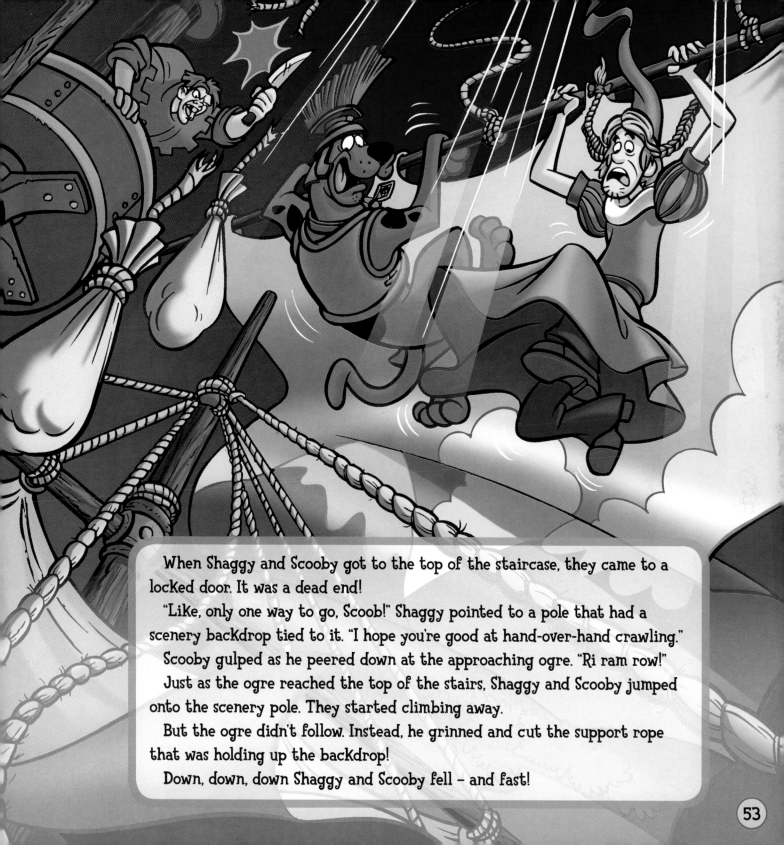

When Shaggy and Scooby got to the top of the staircase, they came to a locked door. It was a dead end!

"Like, only one way to go, Scoob!" Shaggy pointed to a pole that had a scenery backdrop tied to it. "I hope you're good at hand-over-hand crawling."

Scooby gulped as he peered down at the approaching ogre. "Ri ram row!"

Just as the ogre reached the top of the stairs, Shaggy and Scooby jumped onto the scenery pole. They started climbing away.

But the ogre didn't follow. Instead, he grinned and cut the support rope that was holding up the backdrop!

Down, down, down Shaggy and Scooby fell – and fast!

"Good-bye, Scoob, old pal!" Shaggy sniffled. "Like, it looks like splatsville for us!"

"Roh-roh-roh!" Scooby cried.

Then, a miraculous thing happened. Scooby-Doo and Shaggy hit the sail of the Viking boat onstage. The silk of the sail acted like a slide. They glided smoothly toward the bottom!

"Now that's more like it," cheered Shaggy.

"Reah! Reah!" Scooby nodded happily.

But just when they thought they were going to get away, free and clear . . .

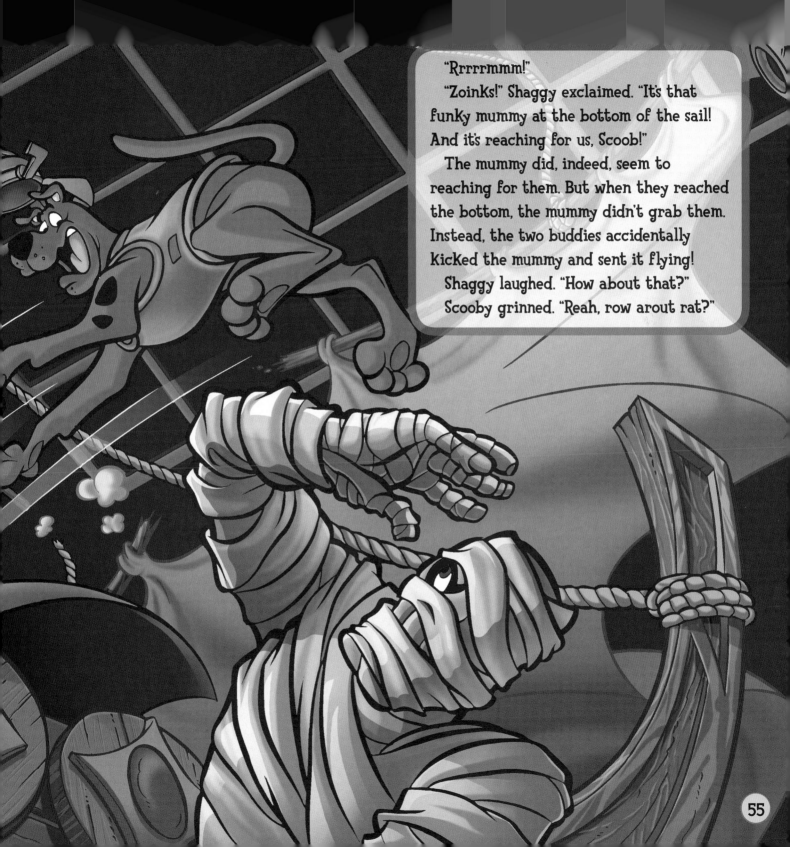

"Rrrrrmmm!"

"Zoinks!" Shaggy exclaimed. "It's that funky mummy at the bottom of the sail! And it's reaching for us, Scoob!"

The mummy did, indeed, seem to reaching for them. But when they reached the bottom, the mummy didn't grab them. Instead, the two buddies accidentally kicked the mummy and sent it flying!

Shaggy laughed. "How about that?"

Scooby grinned. "Reah, row arout rat?"

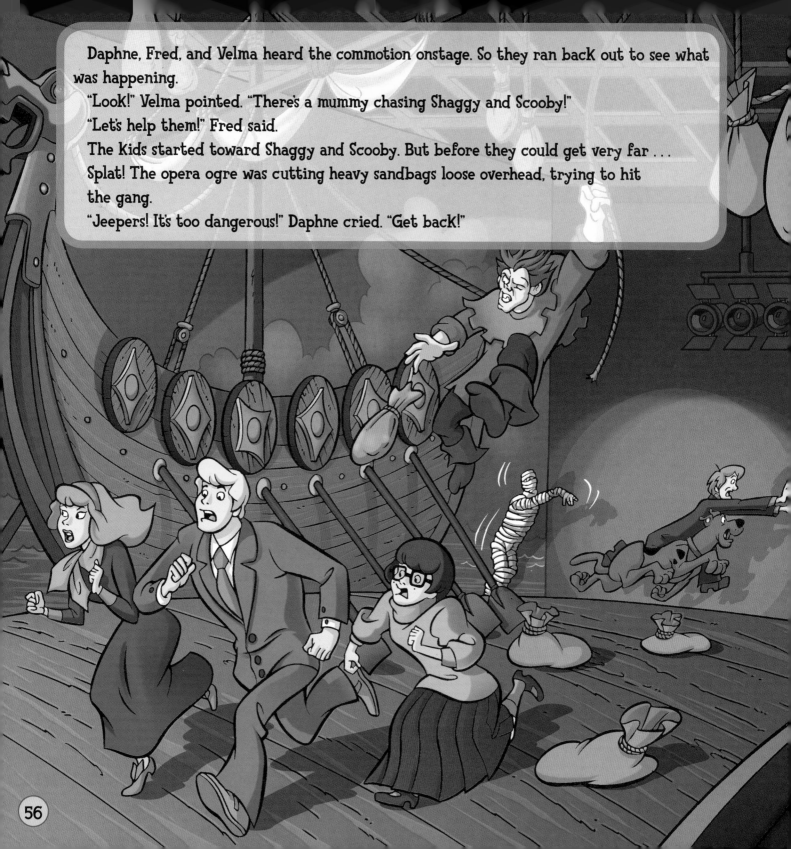

Daphne, Fred, and Velma heard the commotion onstage. So they ran back out to see what was happening.

"Look!" Velma pointed. "There's a mummy chasing Shaggy and Scooby!"

"Let's help them!" Fred said.

The kids started toward Shaggy and Scooby. But before they could get very far . . .

Splat! The opera ogre was cutting heavy sandbags loose overhead, trying to hit the gang.

"Jeepers! It's too dangerous!" Daphne cried. "Get back!"

Shaggy and Scooby were having problems of their own. The mummy chased them into the scenery shop behind the stage. This was the place where the sets were designed, built, and painted.

Crash! Shaggy ran into some old paint cans.

Smash! Scooby skidded into a stack of lumber.

They were so busy running into things, they didn't realize that the mummy was as clumsy as they were.

Bash! The mummy hit its head on a post.

Dashing through the falling sandbags, the rest of the gang joined Shaggy and Scooby in the scenery shop.

"Jinkies! What's all the noise in here?" Velma wondered.

"Like, that crazy mummy is trying to grab us and put one of its creepy curses on us!" Shaggy said.

"Reah, reepy rurses!" Scooby nodded.

"Well, I don't think this mummy can do much to you guys right now," Fred said, examining the unconscious mummy. "It's out cold!"

Just then, Velma made an interesting discovery.

"Hey, look!" she exclaimed. "It's not a real torch at all! It's just a prop made from cellophane and wood, with a tiny light and fan inside!"

"And this is a machine that makes artificial fog and smoke," said Fred. "I think I know what's been going on here."

The kids began to realize that everything was not what it seemed onstage. In fact, Shaggy and Scooby found that out the hard way when they bit into some legs of lamb made out of painted foam!

"Well, two can play at that game," Fred said. "Listen, gang. I've got an idea. . . ."

A short time later, Shaggy and Scooby were back onstage. They were pretending to be Romeo and Juliet.

"I sure hope this works," Shaggy said nervously.

"Rhat right rhough ronder rindow reaks?" Scooby said to Shaggy, playing along.

But the ploy worked. For, just then, the opera ogre appeared, swinging down to get them — just like they wanted!

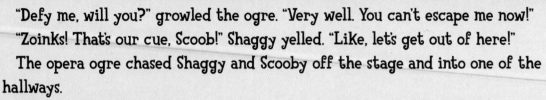

"Defy me, will you?" growled the ogre. "Very well. You can't escape me now!"

"Zoinks! That's our cue, Scoob!" Shaggy yelled. "Like, let's get out of here!"

The opera ogre chased Shaggy and Scooby off the stage and into one of the hallways.

"Relp! Relp!" Scooby cried.

"Like, just keep running, Scoob!" Shaggy huffed. "If we stop, he'll get us!"

"Oh, I'll get you, I will," sneered the ogre. "And your little dog, too!"

Just when it looked like the ogre was going to nab them for sure, Shaggy and Scooby veered suddenly to one side.

Before the ogre could change direction, he smashed through a canvas wall. He didn't notice it because it was painted to look just like the hallway!

Fred was waiting on the other side. When the ogre crashed through, Fred tied him up as neat as you please!

"Like, that's one snazzy special effect!" Shaggy laughed.

"Ruh-huh!" Scooby agreed.

"Now let's see who this opera ogre really is." Fred ripped off the ogre's mask.

"It's that actor, William Bluster!"

"And the mummy is the missing star, Paul Noble!" Daphne exclaimed. "He wasn't trying to get us. He was just asking us to help untie him!"

"I'll bet Bluster kidnapped him," Velma added.

"Yeah! And with Paul Noble out of the way, they would've let me play his part!" growled William Bluster. "The plan would've worked, too, if it weren't for you nosy kids and your dog!"

Just then, Mr. Samuels ran in with the police to take Bluster away.

"Thanks for solving the mystery, Kids!" Mr. Samuels said. "What can I do to repay you?"

"Well, there is one thing." Shaggy smiled at Scooby.

"Reah! Reah!" said Scooby excitedly.

Later, the audience was back in their seats. The opera began with Paul Noble in the lead, just where he belonged. Only now there were two new members in the Viking chorus – Scooby and Shaggy!

"Like, this is the grooviest reward of all!" Shaggy said.

And even in the last row, you could hear Scooby loud and clear when he sang out, "Scooby-Dooby-Doo!"

SCOOBY-DOO IN JUNGLE JEOPARDY

Scooby-Doo and his pals from Mystery, Inc. were visiting Central America. One of Daphne's teachers, Professor Peabody, was an expert in archaeology, the science of uncovering ancient objects buried a long time ago. He was involved with a lot of other scientists in a dig deep in the jungle, and he had invited the kids to join him.

"Daphne!" Professor Peabody greeted them warmly. "I'm so glad you and your friends are here! The expedition is about to begin."

"What are we looking for, professor?" Daphne asked as they ventured into the lush jungle.

"I've heard legends from the local natives about an undiscovered Mayan pyramid around here," the professor explained. "The other scientists think I'm an old fool on a wild goose chase."

"Like, professor, I don't see a pyramid, but there's some sort of old blocky place over there!" Shaggy pointed to a spot through trees and vines. An ancient building was barely visible.

The professor was overjoyed. "My dear boy, that is a pyramid! A Mayan pyramid! You found it!"

Their happy mood was soon cut short, however. The pyramid had a guardian – a fierce, catlike creature that came out snarling at them! And as it snarled, a volcano erupted!

Scooby-Doo was ready to attack the creature. He didn't like mean cats, no matter how big they were!

"Scooby, this is the first time we've had to convince you to run away," Fred said. "But we'd better retreat and think about this!"

They ran, with the snarling cat creature following right behind. Luckily, about a quarter mile from the scientists' camp, the creature stopped chasing them.

When Professor Peabody and the gang told the other scientists what they'd seen, they all laughed.

"It figures you'd find some kids to believe your crackpot theories," said a scientist named McGurty.

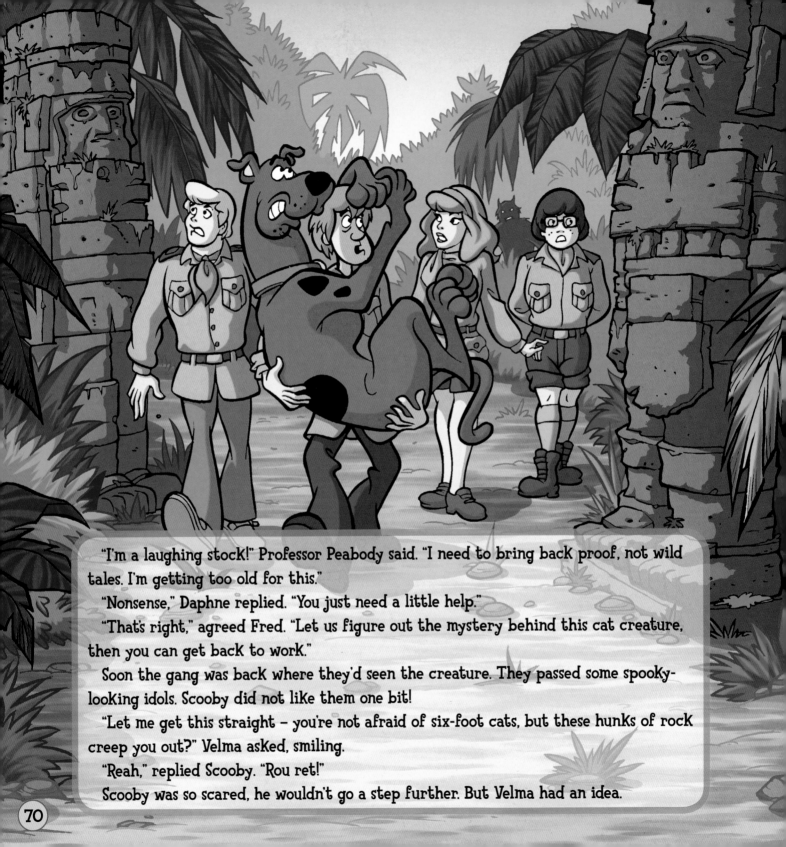

"I'm a laughing stock!" Professor Peabody said. "I need to bring back proof, not wild tales. I'm getting too old for this."

"Nonsense," Daphne replied. "You just need a little help."

"That's right," agreed Fred. "Let us figure out the mystery behind this cat creature, then you can get back to work."

Soon the gang was back where they'd seen the creature. They passed some spooky-looking idols. Scooby did not like them one bit!

"Let me get this straight – you're not afraid of six-foot cats, but these hunks of rock creep you out?" Velma asked, smiling.

"Reah," replied Scooby. "Rou ret!"

Scooby was so scared, he wouldn't go a step further. But Velma had an idea.

"Wow, look at all the fresh fruit on the trees!" she said. "Sure looks yummy!"

"You know, Scoob, Velma's right." Shaggy smacked his lips. "Like, those goodies look ripe for the picking!"

"Reah, reah!" Scooby licked his own lips.

Scooby and Shaggy filled their arms with all kinds of fruit. Soon they couldn't see where they were going!

"Look out!" cried the others. But it was too late!

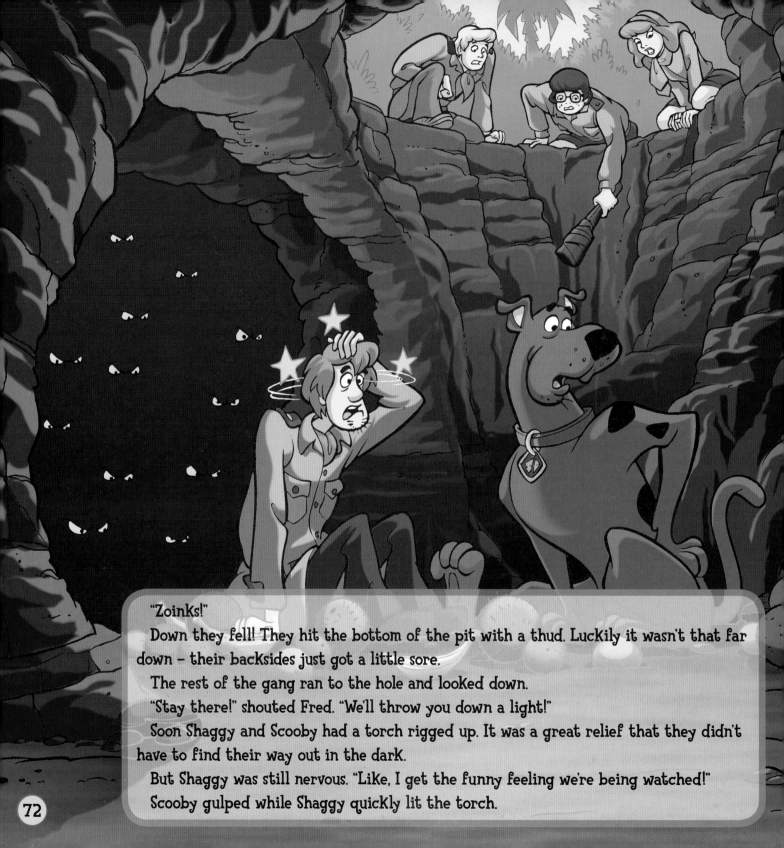

"Zoinks!"

Down they fell! They hit the bottom of the pit with a thud. Luckily it wasn't that far down – their backsides just got a little sore.

The rest of the gang ran to the hole and looked down.

"Stay there!" shouted Fred. "We'll throw you down a light!"

Soon Shaggy and Scooby had a torch rigged up. It was a great relief that they didn't have to find their way out in the dark.

But Shaggy was still nervous. "Like, I get the funny feeling we're being watched!"

Scooby gulped while Shaggy quickly lit the torch.

Suddenly, they were surrounded by bats! Vampire bats! The torch light had startled the sleeping creatures and sent them swarming through the cave. When the bats saw the yummy fruit on the ground, they just had to bite into it.

The sight of the bats' sharp teeth biting into the fruit sent Shaggy and Scooby into a panic.

"Zoinks!" cried Shaggy. "Like, let's get out of here fast, before we're next on the menu!"

Scooby nodded. "Real rast!"

They ran deeper into the cave, getting more and more lost.

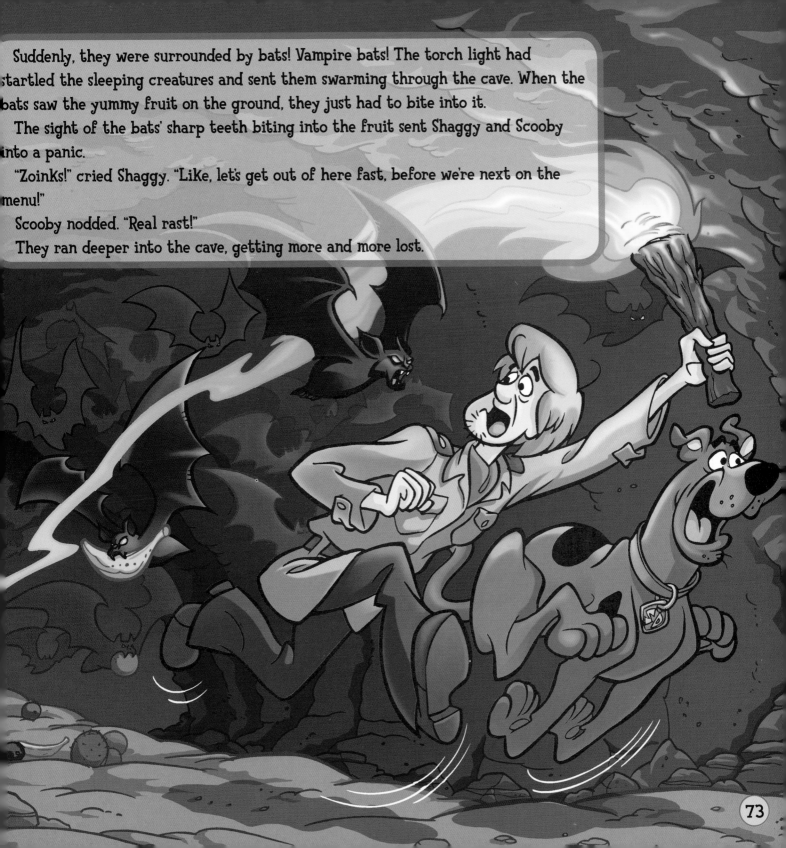

"Shaggy! Scooby! Don't run away!" Velma called. "The bats won't hurt you!"

"It's too late. They're gone!" Fred said. "Let's climb down after them."

But before they could, Velma made an interesting discovery. "Hey, this cave entrance looks like it leads down to the same place!" she said to the others. "Let's go!"

"I'd like it a lot more if the cave didn't look like a cat," Daphne said, shuddering.

Little did they know they were being watched by a pair of eyes. Cat's eyes!

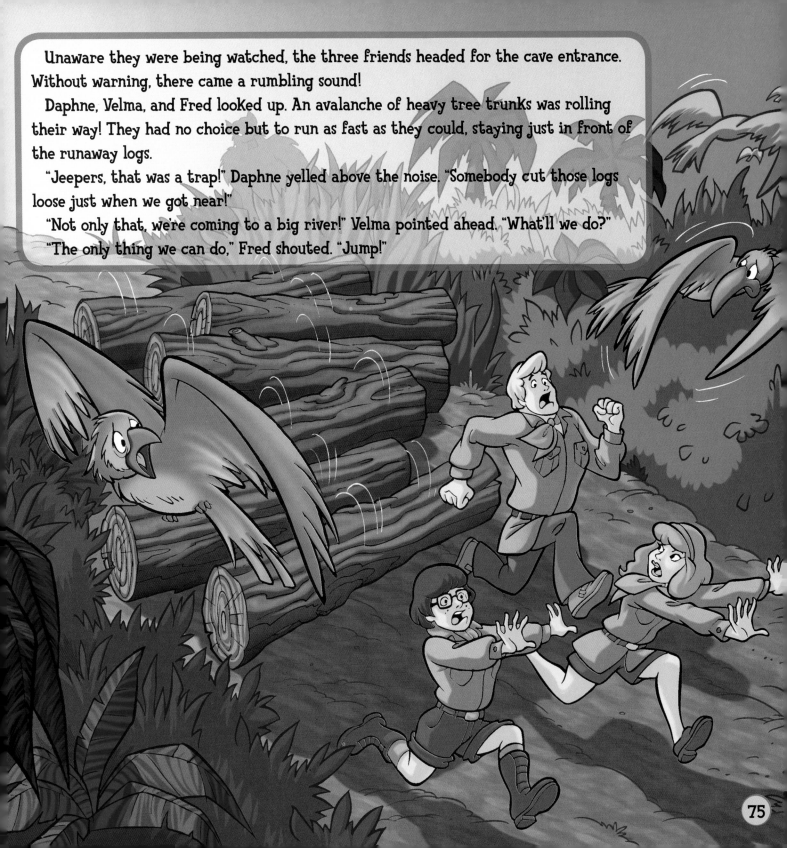

Unaware they were being watched, the three friends headed for the cave entrance. Without warning, there came a rumbling sound!

Daphne, Velma, and Fred looked up. An avalanche of heavy tree trunks was rolling their way! They had no choice but to run as fast as they could, staying just in front of the runaway logs.

"Jeepers, that was a trap!" Daphne yelled above the noise. "Somebody cut those logs loose just when we got near!"

"Not only that, we're coming to a big river!" Velma pointed ahead. "What'll we do?"

"The only thing we can do," Fred shouted. "Jump!"

They jumped into the swiftly moving river and were carried away by the strong current.

Splash! The logs rolled into the river behind them.

"Jinkies! Grab hold of a log and hang on!" Velma cried.

They quickly climbed aboard a sturdy trunk and looked around. That made them feel better – for a minute. Then they heard it.

There was a roaring waterfall up ahead!

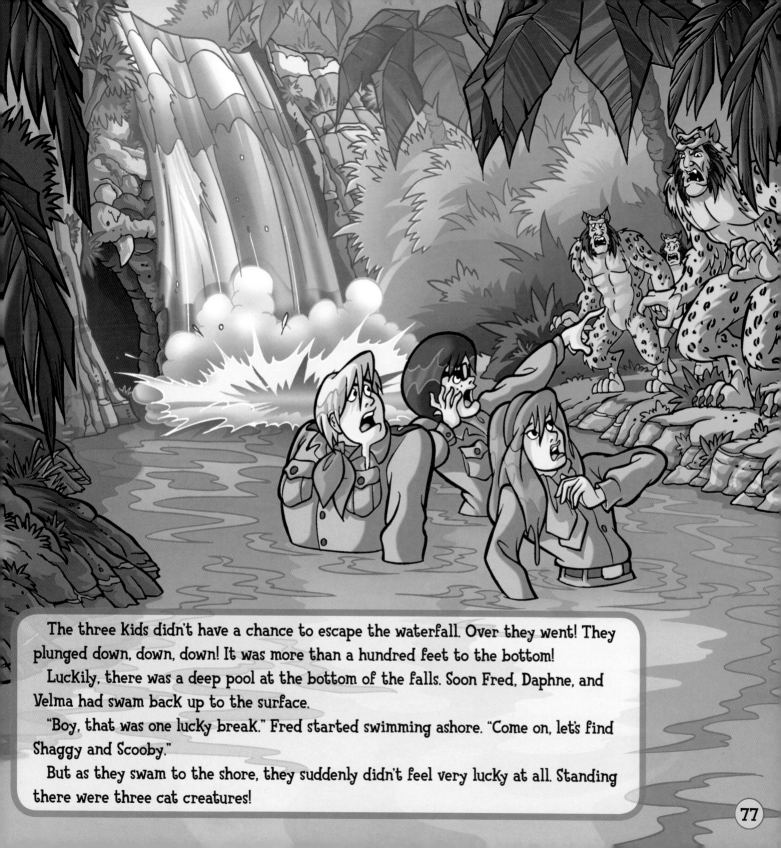

The three kids didn't have a chance to escape the waterfall. Over they went! They plunged down, down, down! It was more than a hundred feet to the bottom!

Luckily, there was a deep pool at the bottom of the falls. Soon Fred, Daphne, and Velma had swam back up to the surface.

"Boy, that was one lucky break." Fred started swimming ashore. "Come on, let's find Shaggy and Scooby."

But as they swam to the shore, they suddenly didn't feel very lucky at all. Standing there were three cat creatures!

Meanwhile, Shaggy and Scooby were deep underground, trying to find their way out. The torch helped a lot, but they could only see a few feet in front of them.

As they crept along, Shaggy kept hearing a funny hissing noise. "Like, say, Scoob, do you hear that?" Shaggy asked. "It sounds like someone left the gas on."

Scooby listened. Then he gulped. "Raggy! Rot ras!" Scooby cried. "Rakes!"

Shaggy laughed. "Like, don't be silly, Scoob. Rakes don't hiss!"

Then Shaggy held the torch up higher. Right in front of them were hundreds of squirming, crawly creatures.

"Zoinks!" Shaggy yelled. "You meant snakes!"

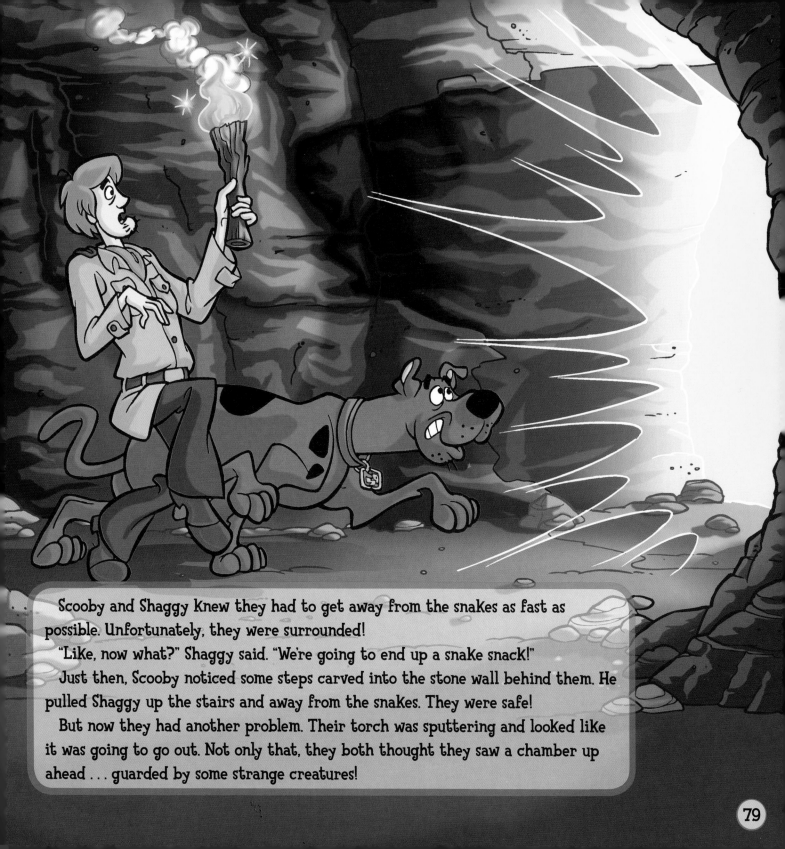

Scooby and Shaggy knew they had to get away from the snakes as fast as possible. Unfortunately, they were surrounded!

"Like, now what?" Shaggy said. "We're going to end up a snake snack!"

Just then, Scooby noticed some steps carved into the stone wall behind them. He pulled Shaggy up the stairs and away from the snakes. They were safe!

But now they had another problem. Their torch was sputtering and looked like it was going to go out. Not only that, they both thought they saw a chamber up ahead . . . guarded by some strange creatures!

Finally, their torch went out. At first Shaggy and Scooby were terrified. Then they realized they could still see! Light was coming from the chamber ahead.

They quietly sneaked up to the chamber's entrance. Whew! The shadows they'd seen weren't creatures after all, just more stone idols.

When they looked around, their mouths dropped wide open. The entire chamber was an ancient Mayan temple!

Scooby was just about to whoop with relief! But Shaggy quickly put his hand over Scooby's mouth.

"Like, quiet, Scoob!" Shaggy warned in a whisper. "Somebody lives here. Who do you think lit those torches?"

"Roh, right." Scooby was suddenly wide-eyed. "Rorry, Raggy."

"Like, let's take a look around – quietly!" Shaggy replied.

Shaggy and Scooby didn't have much of a chance to explore the chamber. Behind them, they heard the sound of footsteps approaching. The two friends quickly hid behind one of the huge idols.

They couldn't believe their eyes when they saw who'd entered!

"Zoinks!" whispered Shaggy. "It's those cat creeps! And they've got Fred and the girls!"

"Grrrrrr," Scooby growled. He really didn't like cats – or creepy cat creatures. And now they had his friends!

"Like, it's nice you want to save our friends, Scoob," Shaggy said, holding Scooby back. "But let's wait for a better chance – like maybe when we have an army with us!"

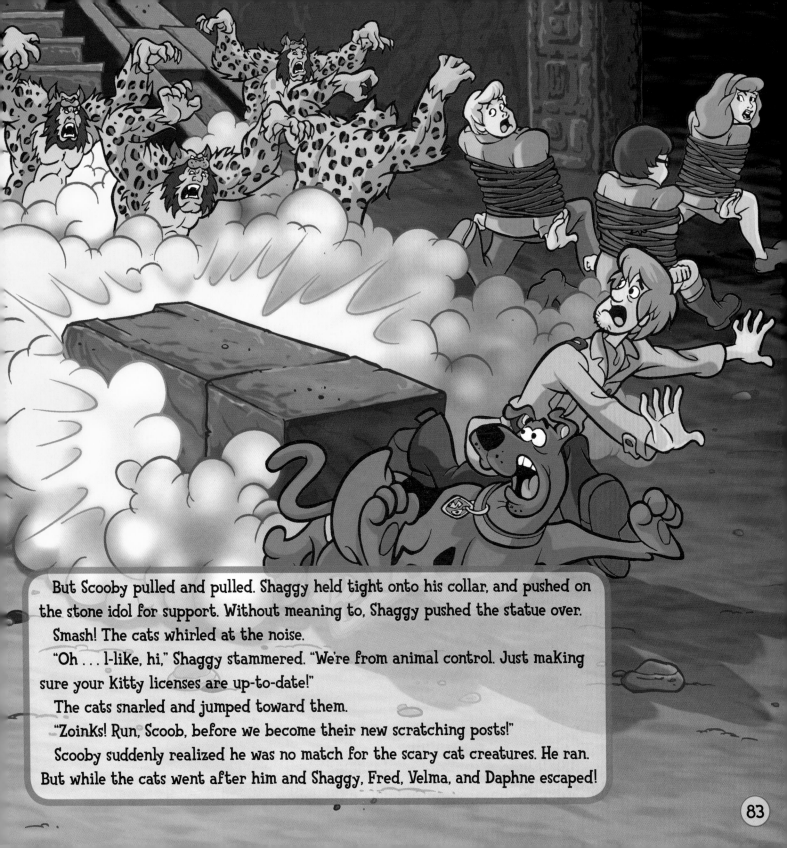

But Scooby pulled and pulled. Shaggy held tight onto his collar, and pushed on the stone idol for support. Without meaning to, Shaggy pushed the statue over.

Smash! The cats whirled at the noise.

"Oh . . . l-like, hi," Shaggy stammered. "We're from animal control. Just making sure your kitty licenses are up-to-date!"

The cats snarled and jumped toward them.

"Zoinks! Run, Scoob, before we become their new scratching posts!"

Scooby suddenly realized he was no match for the scary cat creatures. He ran. But while the cats went after him and Shaggy, Fred, Velma, and Daphne escaped!

The three friends cut their bindings away on a sharp rock. Then they went searching for Scooby and Shaggy.

They found them hiding in a cave with crystal in the walls. There were finely grained crystals under their feet, too. Velma reached down and grabbed a handful. She tasted it.

"Just as I thought. We're in an underground salt mine!"

"Like, you ever get the sinking feeling you were . . . sinking?" Shaggy gulped.

It was true. The kids were sinking in the salt! And when the cats found them, it didn't matter. The gang couldn't run because they were stuck in the salt. It was like quicksand!

But the kids had another stroke of luck: Just after their heads went under, they slid a few feet and landed in a big pile of salt.

"Jinkies!" said Velma happily. "There was a hole at the bottom of the salt pit!"

"Come on, gang," Fred said, starting to walk away. "We don't have much time to spare! Let's get out of here."

They all followed Fred through a nearby tunnel. Before long, they found themselves in a gigantic, round chamber with a hole at the top.

"I think we're in the middle of the volcano!" Fred exclaimed. "And it's hollow!"

"Why would this equipment be here if only the cat creatures live in the caves?" Daphne wondered.

"That's a good question, Daphne," Fred answered. "And that's just what we're going to find out. Let's look around!"

They started investigating the equipment, looking for clues. They hadn't gone very far when, unexpectedly, there came a deep rumbling sound.

Scooby looked up. "Rikes! Rit's a ronster!"

"A monster?" said Velma. "Don't be silly – there's no such thing as monsters!"

"Zoinks! Then there's 'no such thing' after us right now!" cried Shaggy. "Get in the cart and let's get out of here!"

Their cart gained speed as it went deeper underground. If they weren't being chased, it would have been fun – like a roller coaster!

Velma turned to look behind. "That's no monster! It's some sort of machine...a steam shovel!"

"Jeepers! And there's a cat creature driving it!" Daphne added.

Luckily, the steam shovel couldn't go very fast. Soon the gang's cart had left it far behind.

"Like, now I'm really confused!" Shaggy said. "Six-foot cats who walk on two legs is one thing, but cats who drive...that's kooky!"

Fred pointed. "Uh-oh, I think we're coming to the end of this ride...fast!"

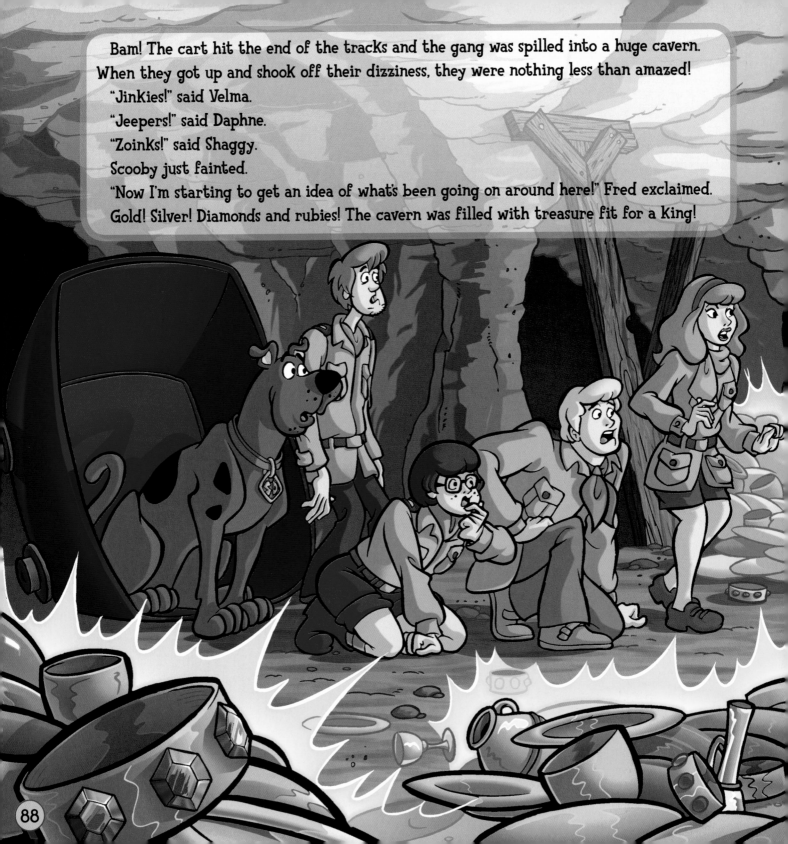

Bam! The cart hit the end of the tracks and the gang was spilled into a huge cavern. When they got up and shook off their dizziness, they were nothing less than amazed!

"Jinkies!" said Velma.

"Jeepers!" said Daphne.

"Zoinks!" said Shaggy.

Scooby just fainted.

"Now I'm starting to get an idea of what's been going on around here!" Fred exclaimed.

Gold! Silver! Diamonds and rubies! The cavern was filled with treasure fit for a king!

"Come on, gang. Those cats will be right behind us," Fred said. "Let's find a way out of here!"

"But, like, aren't we going to do something about this treasure?" asked Shaggy.

"That's exactly what we're going to do," Fred answered, "as soon as we're back up to ground level."

Velma was looking in a different tunnel than the one they'd come through. "This passage looks like it goes all the way up! Wake up, Scooby, and let's get going!"

When they got back up to the surface, Fred explained his plan. As they listened, Scooby and Shaggy became very unhappy.

"Like, no way, Fred!" Shaggy shook his head. "Scoob and I aren't going anywhere near those cats. Like, it's in our contracts...it's called the claws clause!"

"Right!" agreed Scooby.

"Would you do it for some Scooby Snacks?" Velma smiled, waving the tempting treats in front of them.

As usual, Shaggy's and Scooby's stomachs won out over their heads. They soon agreed to do as Fred asked.

Later, at the mouth of the cave, the cat creatures came looking for the kids who had invaded their secret caverns. The cats were shocked when they saw what walked out of the jungle and right up to them.

"Like, howdy!" a cat that looked like Shaggy said. "We're new in the neighborhood, and we were wondering if we could borrow a cup of catnip!"

"Reah!" agreed the cat that looked kind of like a dog.

Velma and Daphne had decorated Shaggy and Scooby to look like cats. They used vines and palm fronds for the costumes.

91

The cat creatures snarled and chased Shaggy and Scooby. The creatures were so distracted by the crazy cat costumes, they didn't notice what the other kids were doing.

As soon as Shaggy and Scooby led the cats away, Fred pulled on a vine. Several logs the gang had collected came rolling down a hill – right at the cats! Now it was their turn to dodge the runaway tree trunks!

The cats snarled and hissed as they tried to avoid the logs. But soon they got away and started chasing Shaggy and Scooby again.

Now Velma went into action. As soon as the cat creatures were under the tree she was hiding behind, Velma pulled on another vine.

Dozens of coconuts came pouring out of the tree! The kids had made a net and filled them with the coconuts. Now they were raining down on the cats and hitting them – hard!

"Like, that's using the old nut, Velma!" Shaggy cheered.

"Reah! Reah!" agreed Scooby happily.

The cats were snarling more than ever. They ran under the tree right next to Velma, Shaggy, and Scooby.

Velma pulled another vine. Another net opened, raining more coconuts on the confused creatures.

The cat creatures were in a panic now. They ran to a clearing where there were no trees, down by the river. When they were close enough, Daphne pulled on a vine that was like a tripwire.

Sploosh! Sploosh!

The cat creatures tripped and went flying into the cold water!

"Help! I can't swim!" yelled one of the creatures.

"Me, neither!" cried another.

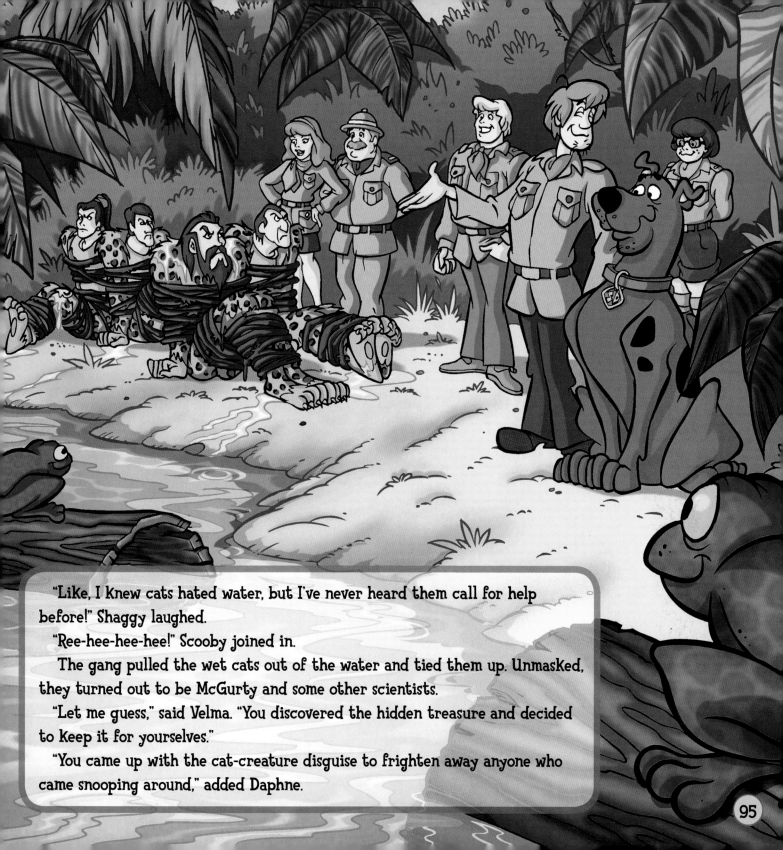

"Like, I knew cats hated water, but I've never heard them call for help before!" Shaggy laughed.

"Ree-hee-hee-hee!" Scooby joined in.

The gang pulled the wet cats out of the water and tied them up. Unmasked, they turned out to be McGurty and some other scientists.

"Let me guess," said Velma. "You discovered the hidden treasure and decided to keep it for yourselves."

"You came up with the cat-creature disguise to frighten away anyone who came snooping around," added Daphne.

"And you used explosives to give the illusion that the volcano was active, so no one would think of looking underground," Fred concluded.

McGurty sneered. "It would've worked, too, if it weren't for you meddling kids and that dog of yours!"

Later, after they'd handed the "cats" over to the authorities, the kids showed Professor Peabody where the Mayan temple was. Then they led him down to the treasure cavern.

"Thanks so much, kids, " said the professor. "I am forever in your debt! Think of all the archaeological research in store for us!"

"Like, I'd rather think of all the Scooby Snacks we have in store for us! Right, Scooby?" Shaggy patted his best pal on the head.

"Scooby-Dooby-Doo!" cheered Scooby.

SCOOBY-DOO AND THE WEIRD WATER PARK

Scooby-Doo and the rest of the Mystery, Inc. gang were on their way across the desert in the Mystery Machine. It was a hot day and everyone was really thirsty. They were all glad when they spied a small town in the distance.

"Hooray!" they cheered when they spotted a roadside refreshment stand.

"Like, I could really go for a cold soda," Shaggy cried.

"Ree, roo!" Scooby-Doo agreed. He nodded and stuck out his tongue. "Bleah!"

As Fred pulled the Mystery Machine off the highway, the gang noticed some sad-looking kids sitting by the stand. It looked like the owner was mad at them.

"You kids are driving me crazy! You're always under my feet," Mr. Reed, the stand owner, growled at the kids. "Find some other place to go."

"Like, why don't you kids beat the heat at that groovy water park over there?" Fred asked.

One boy looked up sadly and said, "We can't. That's my dad's place, and he had to shut it down."

"But why?" asked Daphne. "You'd think it would be a very popular spot in a hot place like this!"

"It's closed because it's haunted," a girl said in a quiet voice. "Haunted by spooky water monsters."

"Ha-ha-haunted?" Shaggy said with a gulp.

"Rooky water ronsters?" Scooby whimpered.

"That's right, water monsters!" Mr. Reed grumbled. "They're evil spirits that sometimes possess watery places!"

"The water monsters are half man and half fish," the boy told the gang, his eyes wide. "They are white like ghosts and they have sharp teeth!"

"Ghosts are bad for business!" Mr. Reed complained.

"Don't worry, everyone, we'll get to the bottom of this," Fred said, leading the gang into the park. "If there's one thing I love, it's a good mystery."

"Zoinks! Like, if there's one thing I don't love, it's ghosts!" Shaggy cried.

Suddenly, Scooby's nose sniffed wildly and his tail stuck straight up into the air like an antenna. Poing!

Shaggy was sniffing, too. "Like, somebody's having a barbecue inside the water park!" he said excitedly.

"Reah! Reah! Rarbecue!" Scooby exclaimed.

THE MEGA JAMMER

THE WATER ROCKET

THE DUNK AND SPIN

Scooby and Shaggy knew they were getting close to the delicious-smelling barbecue, but they couldn't find it. They checked everywhere. Shaggy yanked open a door, then turned as white as a ghost. Without warning, a scary water creature jumped out at them!

"Grrr!" it growled as it reached for them!

"Zoinks! Let's get out of here, Scoob!" Shaggy shouted. "Like, I think I just lost my appetite for barbecue – especially if we're on the menu!"

Shaggy and Scooby raced into a nearby tunnel. It was the water control centre for the park – and it came to a dead end!

"Grrr!" The creature was gaining on them.

"Like, no way to go but up, Scoob!" Shaggy said. "Come on!"

Shaggy climbed up the ladder in a flash. But Scooby wasn't getting anywhere. He was climbing the spokes of a valve wheel, not the ladder! The wheel turned around and around.

"Rooooh!" Scooby-Doo wailed.

Meanwhile, Fred, Daphne, and Velma were checking out the park from above.

"Let's see if we can spot those evil monsters," Fred said.

"Wait, I think I hear something rumbling," Daphne told them. "And it's coming this way!"

Suddenly, a huge surge of water came rushing down the slide. Whoosh! The water caught the kids and carried them away at full speed.

Oh, no! Scooby-Doo had accidentally turned on all the park's water rides!

Soon the gang found themselves being swept down a twisting tube.

"Jinkies! I like water parks as much as anyone!" Velma shouted. "But I wish I'd had time to put on my bathing suit first!"

Down, down, down they sped – through the slide, around crazy turns and dizzying spirals. (Actually, it was kind of fun!)

Then, just as suddenly as it had begun, the ride ended. The kids found themselves washed into a beautiful lagoon. Splash!

Daphne was not happy. "Just look at my hair!" she complained.

"Never mind your hair. Where are my glasses?" Velma asked. "Oh, here they are."

As Velma slid on her specs, she spotted the gang's first clue. There was a strange-looking truck parked next to the lagoon.

"Jeepers," said Daphne. "What's all that equipment in the back of that van? It looks like it's for scientific testing."

Fred nodded. "It is. I've seen that kind of equipment before. It's for locating and testing underground water."

But before they could investigate further, the kids got an unpleasant surprise. A creature from the deep jumped out from behind the truck, growled, and lunged right at them!

At the same time, Shaggy and Scooby were tiptoeing quietly through a dark corridor under the park.

"It looks like we lost that growling ghoulie, Scoob," Shaggy whispered. "Like, I think we're safe."

"Roh boy!" Scooby said happily.

But they quickly changed their minds! A giant octopus with big, ugly eyes and sharp, pointy teeth appeared in front of them. It grabbed at them with a long, slimy tentacle!

Right away, the guys knew they were in trouble. Water was spraying from the walls, filling the entire chamber. Before long, Shag and Scoob had to dog-paddle to keep their heads above water.

Then suddenly, the water was propelling them upward. They looked up – and there was no ceiling, just a long tunnel going up and up!

The two friends hugged each other and gulped.

Scooby and Shaggy shot out the top of the park's volcano. It was like being fired from a water cannon! They were so high up, they could see everything.

"Zoinks! Look, Scoob, there's another monster chasing the rest of the gang!" Shaggy shouted.

But they didn't have time to worry about the others now. For, as fast as they'd gone up, they were now coming down!

Luckily, Shaggy and Scooby landed in the volcano's river. It carried them over churning water-falls down to the lagoon at the bottom. They forgot to be scared – they were having too much fun!

"Like, cowabunga, River Doggie!" Shaggy shouted happily. "Ride those rapids, Scoob!"

"Ree-hee-hee!" Scooby laughed.

Shaggy and Scooby finally came to a gentle stop in the lagoon.

"Man, that was one wild ride!" Shaggy said.

"Reah! Rild!" Scooby-Doo nodded.

"We'd better go find the others," Shaggy suddenly remembered. "They looked like they could use some help!"

The two friends didn't realize it, but at that very moment, they needed help, too!

Close by, Fred, Daphne, and Velma were hiding from the water monsters. Now there were two creatures from the deep chasing after them!

"Those creatures sure are protective of that truck," Velma said. "It must be a very important clue."

Fred noticed an office door. "Let's hide in here and see if we can figure out this mystery!" he said.

"Hmm," Fred said. "This place doesn't look deserted. In fact, it looks like someone works here every day!"

"I found another clue," Velma said, holding up some blueprints. "I'm beginning to get an idea about what's going on around here."

Before Velma could explain, there was a loud banging on the door. The kids jumped.

"Uh-oh. I think those creatures have found us!" Daphne cried.

But it wasn't the water monsters pounding on the door. It was Shaggy and Scooby-Doo!

They were in big trouble! The giant octopus had found them again, and it was trying to wrap them up in its slimy tentacles.

"Like, let us in!" Shaggy shouted.

"Rellllp!" Scooby cried.

Shaggy and Scooby slammed the door before the enormous octopus could reach inside.

"This is no good," Velma said. "That's the only door in or out. We've got to go find more clues if we're going to solve this mystery."

"Like, not me!" Shaggy whimpered. "I'm staying right here, where it's octopus-free!"

"I know what we can do!" Fred said. He pointed to a vent in the wall. "This vent is big enough for us to crawl through. Let's go!"

They all began crawling into the vent. But before Velma climbed in, she spotted another clue. It was a remote control.

Once the gang had crawled to safety, Fred had an idea. "Shaggy and Scooby, you take this hose," he said. "Try to attract the creatures' attention. When you signal, we'll turn on the water full blast. Hose the monsters into that net and we'll wrap them up!"

"Ruh-uh!" Scooby shook his head from side to side.

"Like, no way, Fred," Shaggy said. "We're not going anywhere near those fishy freaks!"

"Would you do it for a handful of Scooby Snacks?" Velma said, holding the treats in the air. "They're nacho-flavoured!"

Shaggy and Scoob couldn't resist Scooby Snacks – especially nacho ones! Soon they were munching happily as they headed off to hunt for the water monsters.

They hadn't gone far when they made a lucky discovery. It was the barbecue they had smelled earlier!

"Like, my compliments to the chef, whoever he is," Shaggy said between bites. Scooby smiled, nodded, and kept chewing.

"Turn on the hose! The hose!" Shaggy yelled as they backed away from the angry creatures.

"Rhe rose! Rhe rose!" Scooby joined in.

But the hose filled with pressure too quickly, and Shaggy and Scooby were lifted off the ground and into the air!

"Too much pressure! Too much!" Shaggy yelled.

"Roo ruch! Roo ruch!" Scooby cried.

Shaggy and Scooby hung onto the wild hose with all their might. It shot back and forth through the air like a bucking bronco.

Fred, Daphne, and Velma tried to turn down the water pressure, but the valve wouldn't budge.

"I've got bad news, girls," Fred said. "This valve is stuck."

"I've got worse news," Daphne replied. "Those creatures are coming after us now!"

But before the monsters could get to the others, Scooby and Shaggy came down again. As they fell, the hose wrapped around the monsters, knotting them up so they couldn't get loose. Scooby and Shaggy had saved the day!

"You couldn't have done better if you were cowboys in a rodeo!" Fred said with a grin as he finally managed to turn off the hose.

All the kids laughed. But then . . .

The snarling, slimy octopus returned!

"Roh, no!" Scooby yelled. He jumped into Shaggy's arms. Everyone was terrified!

Everyone but Velma.

She calmly walked over to one of their captives and took something away from it. It was a remote control! She twisted a knob, and the giant octopus disappeared!

"Like, I don't get it," said Shaggy. "What happened to the big ugly-pus?"

"It was just a hologram," Velma explained. She pointed to a projector up on the water park mountain.

"And these creatures are just the soda stand owner, Mr. Reed, and a couple of his cronies," Fred said.

"According to the blueprints in the office, there's a big supply of underground water beneath the park," Velma continued. "These crooks wanted to develop this land and build a city where they could control all the water."

"That's why they scared everyone away," Daphne said.

"We would have gotten away with it, too, if it weren't for you meddling kids and your dog," muttered Mr. Reed.

It wasn't long before the water park reopened for the town to enjoy. Matt, Amanda, and Ronnie invited Scooby and the gang back for a big party. They had fun in the sun all day long, splashing in the cool water and sliding down the slides!

"Thanks for saving our park," Matt's dad said to the gang. "As far as I'm concerned, you've all got free lifetime memberships here!"

"Rooby-Doobie-Doo!" cheered Scooby.

SCOOBY-DOO AND THE PHANTOM COWBOY

"Yee-haw!" Shaggy cheered, waving his cowboy hat around. "I'm, like, an old cowhand from the Rio Grande, y'all!"

"Ree-raw!" Scooby-Doo joined in, spinning his lasso.

Scooby and his friends from Mystery, Inc. were headed to Phantom Gulch, a real-life western ghost town that had been turned into a theme park.

WELCOME TO PHANTOM GULCH

CLOSED FOR GOOD!

"Jeepers!" Daphne exclaimed. "Where is everybody?"

The gang didn't have to search for long. The remaining citizens of Phantom Gulch were hiding behind the general store. They were about to leave town for good.

"Sorry, folks!" said the town's sheriff, Matt Taff. "Some kind of a ghost has been chasing everyone out of Phantom Gulch. He won't leave us be!"

"That Phantom Cowboy is one mean feller!" Gertie, the owner of the saloon, said, scowling. "And if you know what's good for you, you'll skeedaddle, too!"

"G-g-ghost?" gulped Shaggy.

"Rhantom Rowboy? Roh, ro!" Scooby didn't like the sound of that!

"The Phantom Cowboy has been bothering us for a couple months. We had the worst haunting a few days ago, I reckon," explained Sheriff Matt.

Sheriff Matt said that the creepy cowboy rode atop a wild, snorting, ghost buffalo! He screamed like a crazy prairie coyote during a full moon. The visitors were so scared, they all left in a hurry and no one had come back since.

"You can't have a tourist attraction without tourists," Sheriff Matt said sadly. "The owners of the town had to close down Phantom Gulch and sell the land to the rancher next door. Now we're all out of work, thanks to that spooky sidewinder!"

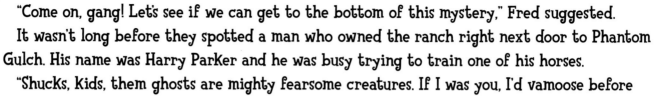

"Come on, gang! Let's see if we can get to the bottom of this mystery," Fred suggested.

It wasn't long before they spotted a man who owned the ranch right next door to Phantom Gulch. His name was Harry Parker and he was busy trying to train one of his horses.

"Shucks, kids, them ghosts are mighty fearsome creatures. If I was you, I'd vamoose before they come back again," Mr. Parker exclaimed. "They're always spooking my horses!"

Fred, Shaggy, and Scooby tried to make friends with Mr. Parker's horse. But it snorted and made like it was going to clobber them with its hooves.

"Zoinks! That horse is spooking me!" Shaggy cried.

Despite Mr. Parker's advice, the kids wanted to investigate Phantom Gulch. While the girls went to the courthouse to look for clues, the boys decided to check out the saloon. But on the way there, Scooby spotted something that really scared him.

"Roast racks!" Scooby gulped, grabbed Shaggy, and pointed nervously. "Roast racks! Roast racks!"

"Like, racks of roasts, Scooby?" Shaggy laughed. "Sounds delicious! Where?"

Fred frowned. "Not racks of roasts, Shaggy. Ghost tracks!"

"Zoinks!" Shaggy exclaimed.

Meanwhile, the girls had found something interesting in the courthouse. After rummaging through an old rolltop desk, they discovered the deed to Phantom Gulch.

"That's strange. According to this, Mr. Parker bought the town last week and sold it to Mega Co. Industries yesterday," Velma said. "Now, why would he do that?"

"Hmm. Good question," Daphne answered. "Let's go ask him." Daphne tried to open the door, but it wouldn't budge. "Jeepers! It's locked!"

Just then, they heard the shuffle of feet on the other side of the door. Then came a low, ominous laugh. Someone – or something – had them trapped inside!

"These are hoof prints, all right," Fred said as he inspected the tracks. "They could belong to the ghost buffalo! Let's see where they lead."

"Like, let's not and say we did," Shaggy said hopefully. "What do you say, Fred, ol' pal?"

"Reah, Red, ol' ral?" Scooby echoed.

Oddly enough, the tracks led right into the saloon. Once they saw there weren't any ghosts there, Shaggy and Scooby thought it was pretty cool to be in a real-life, old west saloon!

"Barkeep!" Shaggy joshed. "We're two tough hombres! Give us a couple of tall root beers, pardner!"

"Ree-hee-hee-hee!" Scooby giggled.

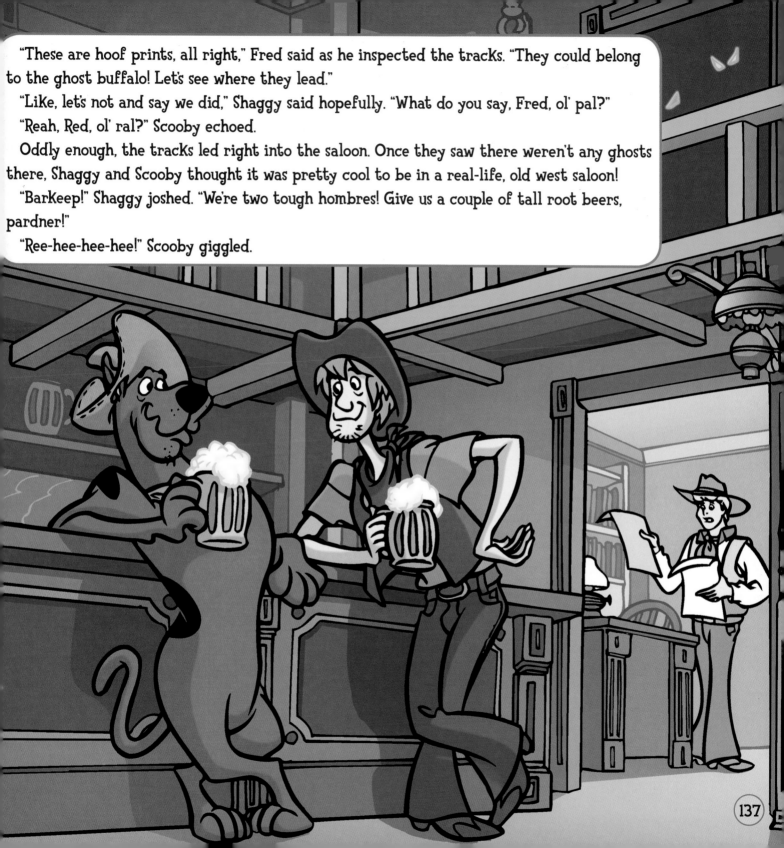

"Shaggy, stop goofing around and take a look upstairs," Fred said, grinning good-naturedly. "Maybe somebody left a clue in one of the boarding rooms."

"Well, shore thing, feller!" Shaggy lifted the brim of his hat just like a real cowboy. Then he swaggered up the stairs to the second level. "Glad t' oblige y'all, tenderfoot!"

Suddenly, the Phantom Cowboy came charging down the staircase riding his rip-snorting buffalo!

"Zoinks! It's the g-g-ghosts! Run!" Shaggy cried. He ran as fast as he could. Meanwhile, the Phantom Cowboy spun a lasso over his head. He was trying to rope Shaggy in!

Shaggy ran down the stairs, across the saloon floor, and out through the double swinging doors. The fearsome ghouls followed close behind!

"Run, Raggy, run!" Scooby hollered.

139

Daphne and Velma listened at the door till they heard the mysterious footsteps walk away. Then they knew they had to escape from the courthouse so they could warn the boys.

Together, the two girls pushed the rolltop desk under a window. Then Daphne climbed on top and up through the window. Velma clambered up after her.

"It's going to be dark soon," Velma said as they crawled out through the window. "I want to find the guys before the sun sets."

Just then, the ghostly cowboy rode by on his buffalo. "Yaaaaaah!" he cried, spurring his creepy creature onward. "Grrrrrowwwl!!"

"Like, heeeelp!" Shaggy was being pulled behind the buffalo, and it looked like a bumpy ride.

"Jinkies!" cried Velma.

Fred and Scooby-Doo were chasing behind the Phantom Cowboy and his buffalo, trying to rescue Shaggy. Just as they were turning a corner and about to disappear from sight, the cowboy turned and pointed at the rest of the gang. "Leave here now!" he called in a booming, eerie voice. "Or I'll come back and get y'all!"

By the time the gang reached the corner, the Phantom Cowboy was gone. And so was Shaggy.

"Jeepers! Now what do we do?" Daphne asked.

"Well, it's getting dark," Velma said. "We can't very well look for Shaggy without some sort of light."

"I'll bet there are some lanterns in there." Fred pointed to an old blacksmith's barn down the street. "Let's take a look."

Sure enough, they found a pair of lanterns and soon had them glowing brightly.

Scooby was feeling very down. His best buddy in the whole world had been whisked away by a spooky desperado riding a buffalo. Velma tried to cheer him with Scooby Snacks, but for once Scooby wasn't in the mood.

"Don't worry, Scooby." Daphne patted him on the head. "Now that we've got light, we're sure to find Shaggy."

Scooby looked determined. "Right!" he barked, jumping to his feet. Soon he was hot on the trail of his kidnapped buddy.

It didn't take long for Scooby to catch Shaggy's scent. He bounded down the street after his friend.

"Look at Scooby go!" Velma said, grinning. "Why, I bet if he lived back in the Old West, he would have been a real trailblazer."

Suddenly, Scooby stopped. He'd found a clue!

"Reanut rutter and relly randrich! Rit's Raggy's!" Scooby declared proudly. Then he pointed down the street. "Rhis ray!"

The gang cautiously followed Scooby to an old bakery and a tailor shop. If Shaggy was inside one of them, then the ghosts could be nearby, too.

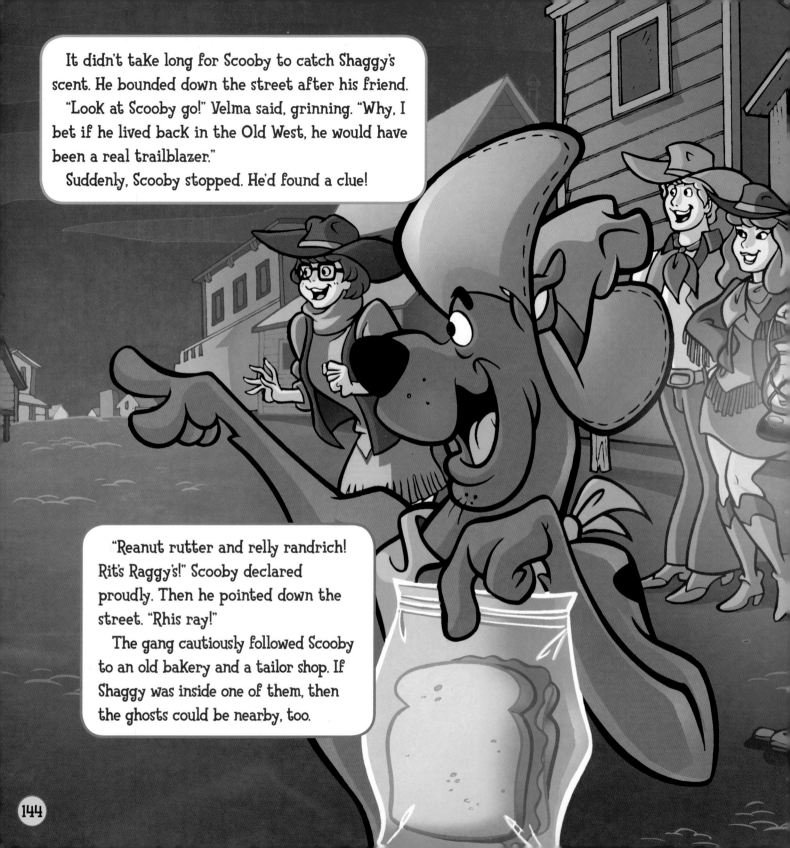

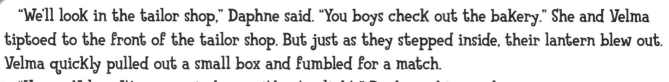

"We'll look in the tailor shop," Daphne said. "You boys check out the bakery." She and Velma tiptoed to the front of the tailor shop. But just as they stepped inside, their lantern blew out. Velma quickly pulled out a small box and fumbled for a match.

"Hurry, Velma. It's creepy in here without a light," Daphne whispered.

Velma struck the match. In the sudden light, Daphne and Velma saw they were surrounded by strange figures.

"Jinkies!" Velma cried. Then they saw that the strangers were just tailors' mannequins. "Whew!"

At the same time, Scooby-Doo and Fred were searching the bakery for any sign of Shaggy. Fred checked the back room while Scooby sniffed the floor near the oven. All the flour and baking powder made him let out a big sneeze.

Just as Scooby sneezed, a big flour sack in the corner jumped. Frowning, Scooby tiptoed to the sack of flour. He sniffed at it. Then he poked at it with his paw. Nervously, Scooby untied the top.

"Zoinks!" cried Shaggy, leaping out, all covered in flour. "Don't hurt me, Mr. Phantom Cowboy, sir!" Scooby's hair stood on end. "Roh, ro! Raggy's a rhost!"

After much yelling and jumping, Scooby realized it was really his friend, not a ghost. They were so happy, they hugged and danced around, getting flour dust everywhere.

"All right, you two," Daphne said, pointing to a nearby water trough. "Time to clean up."

Scooby and Shaggy happily agreed. Then they ran back into the bakery. There were leftover cakes, pies, and other goodies in there.

"Man, like, there's nothing like some good eats after you've had the wits scared out of you!" Shaggy declared, chomping on a bagel.

"Roo raid rit!" agreed Scooby between bites of cake.

147

"Well, it looks like everyone's back to normal." Fred grinned. "Now, let's find those ghosts."
But they didn't have to find the ghosts. The ghosts found them!
Out of the darkness emerged the scary rider on his fearsome buffalo. The kids barely dodged out of the way before the ghosts thundered past. Then the cowboy turned his mount around and headed back for another charge. The gang ran for it.
"Ha ha ha ha ha!" cackled the cowboy as he rode down the main street of Phantom Gulch.
"I'll give y'all one more chance to leave this place! Now go!" Then the ghosts disappeared again.

"Well, it's going to take a lot more than that to scare us away." Daphne frowned. "Right, guys?"

"Like, I don't know…" Shaggy began.

"Right!" agreed Fred. "Let's see if we can follow those buffalo tracks! We need to catch those ghosts when they're not expecting us."

"Zoinks!" groaned Shaggy. "I was afraid you were going to say that!"

Scooby nodded miserably, "Ree, roo!"

The buffalo tracks led the kids out of town and down a dusty road. After a while, they spotted a campfire burning on a hill. When they got close enough to get a good view, they realized the campfire wasn't on a hill - it was built inside a hill!

AUTHENTIC NATIVE AMERICAN PUEBLO

"Man, what a crazy apartment!" Shaggy said.

"That's a pueblo, Shaggy," Velma explained. "Certain Native American tribes used to build pueblos to live in long ago."

"It looks like our ghost friends have moved in," Fred said. "Let's see if they're up for some company."

Long ladders were leaning against the side of the pueblo, so the gang had an easy time climbing up. Fred peeked into the apartment. No one was in sight. He motioned the others forward.

When they were all inside, the gang spread out, searching for clues. Velma found an old mural painted by elders of the tribe that had once lived there.

"This is fascinating," Velma told the gang. "This mural tells of the coming of the settlers and the extinction of the buffalo. According to legend, a mighty phantom will rise up with his ghostly buffalo and curse the descendants of the settlers forever!"

"But if this cowboy is a ghost, why does he need a campfire at night?" Fred pondered. "Something doesn't add up."

"Like, who cares?" Shaggy was hugging Scooby tightly. "Now that we know the Phantom Cowboy and his creepy critter are the curse-ers, let's fly this coop before we become the curse-ees!"

"Reah! Reah!" Scooby nodded.

"Too late!" bellowed a booming voice. The ghoulish cowboy and his stamping, snorting buffalo sidekick appeared out of nowhere.

As quick as a wink, the gang scrambled back down the ladders to the bottom of the pueblo. They thought that they'd lost the ghostly duo. But all of a sudden, the ghouls appeared from behind a huge boulder and the chase was on again!

Back through the desert the cowboy chased them. Back through the town of Phantom Gulch he rode after them, laughing, whooping, and hollering all the while.

In fact, the ghosts didn't let up until they'd chased the kids all the way back to the Mystery Machine. When he thought he had finally scared the gang away, the cowboy reared up on his buffalo and rode off in a cloud of dust.

But Fred and the girls weren't about to give up so easily.

"There's got to be a logical explanation for this Phantom Cowboy mystery!" Velma exclaimed.

"The only way we'll get to the bottom of this is by catching that ghost, and I've got an idea how," Fred declared. He looked at Shaggy and Scooby. "Of course, we'll need some bait."

"Like, no way, Fred!" Shaggy cried. "I've had my fill of creepy cowboy curses for one night!"

"Right!" Scooby stuck out his tongue. "Bleah! Reepy rowboy rurses!"

153

After several minutes of wrangling for Scooby Snacks, Shaggy and Scooby agreed to help catch the ghosts. Velma and Daphne took them back to the tailor shop and dressed them like Old West lawmen.

While Fred and the girls went to set up the trap, Shaggy and Scooby went looking for the Phantom Cowboy and his buffalo. The two ghosts had set up a camp in the desert right outside of town. Taking deep breaths for courage, Shaggy and Scooby moseyed right up to the campfire.

"Howdy, Deputy Scoobert! Do y'all see what I see?" Shaggy said in his best cowboy voice. "A coupla mangy varmints having a weenie-roast without a campfire permit!"

"I think we should run these rascals into the pokey!" Shaggy continued. "Wouldn't y'all agree, Deputy Scoobert?"

"Right, Rarshal Raggy," Scooby answered.

The Phantom Cowboy and his ghost buffalo looked at them in surprise for a minute. Then looks of anger came over their faces. They growled and howled at Shaggy and Scooby.

"Like, on the other hand, maybe we should just let them go with a warning this time," Shaggy called as he turned and bolted away. "Run, Scooby-Doo!"

"Roh-oh-oh!" Scooby cried as he raced away from the campfire.

Scooby-Doo and Shaggy fled through the desert, over brambles and around big boulders. They tried hiding behind cacti and running with the tumbleweeds. But no matter what they did, the Phantom Cowboy and his ghostly buffalo stayed right on their heels.

Finally, with no other choice left, the two friends started climbing a small hill nearby. But it was no use - the ghosts stayed right with them. And Scooby and Shaggy were quickly running out of steam!

When Scooby and Shaggy reached the top of the slope, they realized the hill suddenly ended with a sharp dropoff. They were trapped!

"Oh, no!" Shaggy cried.

This made the Phantom Cowboy laugh with evil delight. "I told y'all to vamoose from these here parts." The ghost grinned. "Now it's too late for you!"

"Like, this is it, old pal," Shaggy said to Scooby. "Happy trails!"

"Ro long, Raggy!" Tears came to Scooby's eyes. "Roh, roo hoo hoo!"

But just as the Phantom Cowboy and the ghost buffalo were about to nab Shaggy and Scooby, the villains fell through a hole in the ground. It was a trap — a hole that Fred, Daphne, and Velma had camouflaged with weeds and grass. The hole was carved into the roof of the pueblo to let the smoke from campfires drift out.

Daphne, Fred, and Velma were waiting underneath the hole with a big net, ready to catch the villains. The Phantom Cowboy and the ghost buffalo dropped right into it, as pretty as you please!

"Now, let's see who was behind this mystery." Fred pulled the mask off the captured Phantom Cowboy.

It was Mr. Parker! He had been pretending to be the Phantom Cowboy all along. The ghost buffalo had actually been his horse in disguise.

"Mr. Parker scared away all the people in Phantom Gulch so he could buy the property real cheap," Velma explained as state troopers arrived to take Mr. Parker away. "Then he sold the town for a huge profit to a big company that wanted to build an even bigger western amusement park."

"I would've gotten away with it, too, if it weren't for you meddlin' kids and your mangy dog!" sneered Parker.

"Once the judge finds out what Parker did, the town will revert back to its rightful owners," Daphne said, smiling.

Not too long after that, the townspeople who worked at Phantom Gulch returned to their old jobs. Soon visitors started coming back and the town was a lively, old western tourist attraction again.

"We can't thank you enough for solving the mystery and saving Phantom Gulch!" said Sheriff Matt gratefully. "You kids are real western heroes!"

"Like, shucks, Sheriff...'tweren't nothin' any real western heroes couldn't have done," Shaggy drawled. "As long as they had a pardner like Scooby-Doo!"

"Scooby-Dooby-Doo!" cheered Scooby.

PHANTOM GULCH

GRAND REOPENING